Other books by
Janet Tashjian

The Marty Frye, Private Eye series:
The Case of the Missing Action Figure
The Case of the Stolen Poodle

The Einstein the Class Hamster series:
Einstein the Class Hamster
Einstein the Class Hamster and the Very Real Game Show
Einstein the Class Hamster Saves the Library

The Sticker Girl series:
Sticker Girl

The My Life series:
My Life as a Book
My Life as a Stuntboy
My Life as a Cartoonist
My Life as a Joke
My Life as a Gamer
My Life as a Ninja

Multiple Choice
Tru Confessions

Janet Tashjian

Sticker Girl

Rules the School

with illustrations by
Inga Wilmink

SQUARE
FISH

Christy Ottaviano Books

Henry Holt and Company ⭐ New York

SQUARE FISH

An imprint of Macmillan Publishing Group, LLC
175 Fifth Avenue, New York, NY 10010
mackids.com

Our books may be purchased in bulk for promotional, educational, or business
use. Please contact your local bookseller or the Macmillan Corporate and
Premium Sales Department at (800) 221-7945 ext. 5442 or by e-mail at
MacmillanSpecialMarkets@macmillan.com.

Library of Congress Cataloging-in-Publication Data

Names: Tashjian, Janet, author. | Wilmink, Inga, illustrator.
Title: Sticker girl rules the school / Janet Tashjian ; with illustrations by
Inga Wilmink.
Description: First edition. | New York : Henry Holt and Company, 2017. |
"Christy Ottaviano Books." | Summary: Martina and Bev find another
sheet of magical stickers, and soon Martina finds herself running for
class president but worrying that she is losing her new friend.
Identifiers: LCCN 2017009675 (print) | LCCN 2017035151 (ebook) |
ISBN 9781627793391 (Ebook) | ISBN 9781250183378 (paperback)
Subjects: | CYAC: Elections—Fiction. | Schools—Fiction. | Best friends—
Fiction. | Friendship—Fiction. | Self-confidence—Fiction. | Stickers—
Fiction. | Magic—Fiction.
Classification: LCC PZ7.T211135 (ebook) | LCC PZ7.T211135 Stg 2017
(print) | DDC [Fic]—dc23
LC record available at https://lccn.loc.gov/2017009675

Originally published in the United States by
Christy Ottaviano Books/Henry Holt and Company
First Square Fish edition, 2018
Book designed by April Ward and Rebecca Syracuse
Square Fish logo designed by Filomena Tuosto

1   3   5   7   9   10   8   6   4   2

LEXILE: 790L

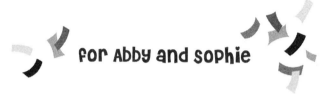

for Abby and Sophie

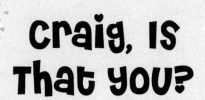

Craig, is That you?

You know how sometimes even the most patient kid practically crawls out of her skin with anticipation? Well, seeing Craig—my funny, grumpy cupcake friend—on the new sheet of stickers gives me that feeling.

I take a deep breath and count to ten.

My friend Bev looks over my shoulder at the sheet of stickers. I'm sure she's thinking the same thing: will *these* stickers be magical too?

"Let me guess. You're trying to decide if you should peel off Craig first, right?" Bev says.

"Especially since one of the *other* stickers is a treasure chest."

To be honest, it's not a tough decision. Even though Craig caused his share of trouble last time, he was pretty fun to have around. But there are only ten stickers, so pacing myself is a must.

Besides Craig, the new stickers are a . . .

♥ girl soccer player

♥ chipmunk ballerina

♥ honeybee with a trumpet

♥ treasure chest

♥ pizza

♥ cell phone

♥ zombie DJ

♥ palette with paint

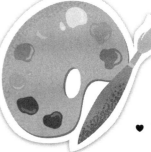

♥ hot-air balloon

3

I just hope this new batch of stickers turns out to be a little less trouble than the last sheet.

"I can't believe you're hesitating," Bev jokes. "You have to use at least ONE while I'm here."

It's not that I don't want to share the magic with Bev—I mean, she rode with me on a Pegasus that was once a sticker. But what if something goes wrong? What if the stickers we just found hidden in my little brother's toy toolbox aren't enchanted like the last batch? Or worse—what if they're evil?

Bev sits down on my bed. "If you don't hurry up and do it, I will," she teases.

She's right. Why am I hesitating? I gently peel my little cupcake friend off the sheet of stickers.

whoosh! POOF! BAM!

Craig immediately appears in my hand, coughing and wheezing.

"Martina! I missed you!"

When Bev whips her head around to see him, I can't help but smile.

This is real.

This is happening.

my stickers are alive— again!

A Pouty Baked good

Since you can't really hug a cupcake, it's a bit awkward showing Craig how happy I am to see him. The last thing I want to do is squish him on his first day back. He remembers Bev and says hello.

There are a million questions I want to ask: Where did he go when the stickers returned to the sheet? Was it like sleeping or being dead? Is there anything he should warn me about BEFORE I peel the stickers off this time? (I may decide to take a pass on the zombie. . . .)

It's as if Craig can read my mind, because he crosses his arms and scowls. "I'm not even here for a minute and you're already wondering what we stickers can do for you! Ever think about what WE might want out of this, Martina? We're the ones who finally get to come alive—you should take OUR needs into consideration. It's just plain DULL sitting on that sheet, waiting to get peeled off!"

Bev claps her hand over her mouth and tries not to laugh.

"He's very opinionated," I say.

As Craig stomps around my desk, tiny crumbs fly off him. I tell him if he doesn't stop getting so upset, he'll be a *mini* cupcake by the end of the day.

"Just keep those monsters away from me."

I don't know what he's talking about until I see my brother James and my dog, Lily, in the hall. James is only two years old and Lily's a Chihuahua, so neither can be categorized as a monster, but I suppose if Craig tastes as good as he looks, everyone's a potential threat.

"Cupcake!" James squeals. "Cupcake talks!"

Lily arches her back and lets out a low growl, so Bev picks her up and rubs her belly. "I can't believe you chose Craig first! Ninety-nine percent of the people in the universe would've taken the treasure chest."

Maybe Bev's right and I'm being too cautious with my magical stickers. Maybe since I've got a friend to hang out with now, their magic will be much more manageable.

I try to hand the sheet of stickers to Bev but she shakes her head. "No way. They probably only work when *you* peel them off."

"There's one way to find out." I continue holding the sheet of stickers out to her.

"I don't think that's such a good idea," Craig says. "There's no telling what will happen if you let everyone in the world share in the magic."

Considering I pretty much have only one or two friends here, Craig's warning is definitely overkill. But his comment does make me realize it might not be smart to tempt fate.

"You're right, Bev—let's peel off the treasure chest." Both of us hover over the sticker as I lift it off the sheet.

whoosh! POOF! BAM!

A chest

overflowing with gold, diamonds, rubies, and emeralds is now in the center of my room. Bev and I stare at the old wooden trunk like a couple of pirates.

Then we scream.

Craig laughs. "It's like you two have never seen a fortune before."

"Probably because we HAVEN'T!" Bev takes

a handful of diamonds and rubies and examines them.

I think about all the coupons my mom cuts out, how many clothes she mends, how many hours my father works at the diner he owns. Suddenly we're rich! This can really change our lives!

Lily sniffs at the gems scattered on the rug while James dives into the chest.

How am I going to explain this windfall to my parents? How are we going to move this trunk? How can I hide this from my brother Eric, who thinks what's mine is his just because he's older?

But most important—WHAT AM I GOING TO DO WITH ALL THESE JEWELS?

wait—what?

Bev and I spend the next hour making lists of things we HAVE to have, then lists of things it'd be NICE to have. (Lily absolutely needs a purple rhinestone collar. She's wanted one for years.)

It's fun having a partner in crime to share my good fortune with, even if Bev insists the booty is officially mine.

We pick up the gems from the floor and return

them to the trunk. Then we go to the garage and find an old piece of plywood to make a table using the treasure chest as a base. We cover the plywood with a piece of flowery fabric Mom made curtains out of, and suddenly there's a pretty table in the center of my room.

Mom does a double take as she walks down the hall. "I like the new table! Where'd you get it?"

I tell her someone up the street put it out on trash day.

"Oh, Marti! You're so much like me, trying to stretch every dollar." She sits on the end of my bed. "But if you need something, honey, just ask."

If Mom only knew about the pile of riches that was under that tablecloth! It takes every bit of self-control not to blurt the news. Wait till Mom realizes one of the first things I plan to do with this money is buy her a new car to replace her old Chevy, which has almost two hundred thousand miles on it.

After Mom leaves to take a phone call, Bev is a nonstop fountain of ideas. "I think we should go to that big bank downtown. Or maybe that jewelry store where my mom got her wedding ring repaired. The owner knows a lot about diamonds."

I try to picture Bev and me dragging a wagon full of jewels all the way downtown.

"You two are BEGGING to get robbed," Craig says. "Just be careful."

"What are we supposed to do, hire an armored car and bodyguards?" I stop and think about the words that just came out of my mouth. My biggest worry before this week was whether I should run for student council, and now I'm talking about hiring security? Maybe this whole treasure thing isn't worth the potential anxiety.

After I grab Dad's wheelie suitcase from the garage, Bev and I take turns guarding the door and filling the suitcase with jewels.

"Here comes your brother," Bev whispers.

"Which one?"

"The troublemaker."

"I still don't know who you mean." I fling the tablecloth back onto the trunk.

As if to answer my question, Eric sticks his pimply face into the room and points to the suitcase.

"Running away?"

"Yeah, as far away from you as I can get." I hope the comment will get rid of him, but Eric just stands there.

"Make sure to take that yippy dog with you."

Bev gives me a look to keep quiet. She's right—this is hardly the time to get into a battle of wits with my brother.

"Well, since you have zero chance of making it in the real world on your own, I'll just put this back." When Eric reaches for the suitcase, Bev and I block it with our bodies. But Eric's too big and reaches across us as if we're hardly there.

He lifts the suitcase up and down like it's

a barbell. "What do you have in here? It weighs a ton!"

"My pet rock collection," Bev says. "Want to see it?"

I'm shocked by Bev's boldness. Suppose Eric says yes?

Instead, he rolls his eyes and puts the suitcase down. "Pet rocks," he mutters. "Totally stupid."

"Eric!" Mom calls. It's like the cavalry just rode in to save the day.

But Eric doesn't move, just continues to stare at the suitcase.

"Ahora!"

"All right already!" Eric heads down the hall to the kitchen.

"Your mom's timing was perfect!" Bev says.

"I don't think that was my mom." I lift my bag from the nightstand; Craig's inside, smiling sheepishly.

"You're welcome," he says.

Bev is confused until I tell her about Craig's awesome ventriloquist skills. What I *don't* tell

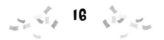

her about is the day last month when I volun-
teered to be her partner on a school project. It
wasn't actually me—Craig was using his voice-
throwing skills then too. Wait—my talking
cupcake friend knows Spanish too?

In fact, there's quite a bit I haven't told Bev—
that sometimes her crazy ideas make me nervous,
that I worry one of her tall tales will get us into
trouble. Or that I wonder if we're only friends
now because she got to ride on the Pegasus
when it came to life. Is she hanging out with me
because she's eager for another adventure, or
does she really like *me*?

It's been a year since my family moved to the
San Fernando Valley, and I'd almost given up
hope for a best friend. These past weeks with
Bev have been *amazing*. I just hope it's a friendship that lasts.

When I hear another voice in the hall, I can
tell it's *not* Craig. It's my dad. How am I going to
explain his suitcase in the middle of my room?

"Ah! There it is!" Dad smiles when he sees

the luggage. "Your abuelita wants to borrow that for her trip with the girls this weekend."

I almost laugh at how my grandmother and her friends who wear dentures and orthopedic shoes still call one another "girls," but I'm too busy trying to come up with an excuse for why Dad can't take the suitcase.

Before we can open our mouths, Dad's already wheeling the suitcase out of the room.

Until he stops. "I must've forgotten to unpack this. It's heavy."

He bends down to open it.

"Dad, no!"

My father ignores me and unzips the bag. "Well, what do we have here?"

The jewels spill onto the floor.

"These are great!" Dad says. "Such deep colors. Where'd you get them?"

Bev and I glance at each other. Who will come up with the better story? I decide on the truth; Dad will find out about the treasure sooner or

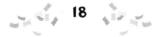

later—it might as well be now.

As I'm about to come clean, Dad holds a glistening sapphire up to the window.

"These remind me so much of the jewels your abuelita used to glue onto the floats for the church pageant." His eyes become wistful. "My friends and I would play pirates and pretend all the jewels were real."

They are real, I want to yell. But just as I'm about to open my mouth, Dad squeezes the sapphire in his hand. The gem immediately breaks into blue dust. "We used to have fun smashing them too."

When he sees our expressions, he laughs and

points to the pile of jewels. "You didn't think these were *real*, did you?"

Bev and I are too stunned to speak. So much for Mom's new car, a closet full of clothes, and—gulp—Lily's rhinestone collar.

What good is a treasure-chest sticker of *fake* jewels? Bev looks as disappointed as I am.

Dad empties the rest of the jewels onto the floor and heads down the hall with the suitcase. "Have fun making necklaces, decorating bracelets, or whatever you girls are doing."

Craig chuckles from behind one of the corduroy pillows on my bed.

"You knew they were fake?" I ask.

"Totally not cool, Craig," Bev adds.

"Honestly, I had no idea. But you have to admit it *is* kind of funny."

For me, it's anything but.

"You still have a talking cupcake," Bev says to cheer me up. "And that's kind of cool."

"KIND OF?" Craig bellows.

I tell him to calm down while Bev and I scoop up our booty of counterfeit jewels.

"So much for our wish list," Bev says.

A sly grin creeps across Craig's chocolate face. "We stickers can be VERY surprising."

To say the least.

student council

At school the next day, I tell my friend Mike that I'm thinking of running for class secretary.

"You're so organized," he says. "Way more than anyone else in our class. You'll be great."

I *am* good with organizing information, but that's not why I decided to run for secretary. I chose that particular position because no one else is running for it.

When Bev approaches us at our lockers, she disagrees. "I think you should run for class president," she suggests. "Craig and I were talking about that yesterday."

"Who's Craig?" Mike asks.

I glare at Bev. She *knows* my magical stickers are top secret, even for Mike. Sure, he rode a Pegasus with us when I had my *last* magical sheet of stickers, but he believed our story about borrowing an animatronic Pegasus from a movie studio. Why is she casually dropping hints about Craig now?

Bev, of course, doesn't miss a beat and tells Mike that Craig is one of our friends from the neighborhood.

"You have to be careful!" I whisper when Mike heads down the hall. "Next thing, you'll be telling him about the fake treasure chest too."

"Hey! There's nothing fake about us stickers!"

I spin around to see where the familiar voice is coming from. Bev grins and opens her bag to reveal Craig.

"I stopped by your house this morning but you'd already left," Bev says. "Craig was making a fuss and I didn't want your mom to hear him, so I took him along."

Craig rolls his eyes. "I was HARDLY making a fuss."

"Promise you'll keep quiet and you can stay." I open my own bag and Craig hops in.

On the way to class, I think about Bev's comment. To be honest, I *did* consider throwing my hat in the presidential ring, but Tommy and Caitlyn are already running. Tommy may be a goofy bull-in-a-china-shop who tells terrible jokes, but he's one of the most popular kids in our grade. Caitlyn's popular AND smart; I like her too. A few months ago, I barely spoke to any of my classmates, so running for a position no one else has signed up for is a good way to test the waters and become more involved in school. Class secretary it is.

When I take my seat, I notice my teacher Ms. Graham's arm is in a cast; she acts out a story about rollerblading in Santa Monica, slipping on some sand, and breaking her humerus.

"There's nothing humorous about breaking your humerus," Tommy calls out.

It's a stupid joke but Tommy gets a laugh anyway.

"Okay—I know school elections are usually in the fall," Ms. Graham says. "But politics is so important to what's going on in the world right now, I don't want to wait that long." She looks over the class. "Who wants to run for student council?"

I look around the room, then slowly raise my hand.

"Martina! What would you like to run for?"

Before I can open my mouth, Craig does a perfect impersonation of me and pipes up, "President!"

Tommy's head whips around. So does Caitlyn's. They're as shocked as I am.

Ms. Graham seems surprised too. "Martina, that's great! It's going to be a fun campaign."

STUDENT COUNCIL BALLOT

CLASS PRESIDENT
TOMMY
CAITLYN
MARTINA

While she writes my name on the white-board, I open my bag and give Craig the evil eye. "You ruin everything!" I whisper.

Craig rolls his buttercream eyes. "Running unopposed is lame. I'm with Bev on this."

When I look over at Bev, she's grinning too. Did my best human friend and best pastry friend just conspire against me?

I'm about to tell Ms. Graham that I actually meant to say I wanted to run for secretary when Samantha sticks her hand in the air.

"I'll run for secretary!" she says.

"Excellent! Though I'm not sure how much of a run it will be. So far you're the only one on the ticket!" Ms. Graham jokes.

That could've been me, I think to myself. *Thanks, Craig!*

Ms. Graham studies the list of candidates. "We still need a treasurer! Going once, going twice . . ."

Now's my chance. I lift my arm to volunteer, but Scott's already shouting, "Me! Me!"

"Okay, Scott. You're on the ballot," Ms. Graham confirms.

"One question," Scott begins. "What's a treasurer?"

"Treasurers are in charge of counting money and budgeting for school activities," Ms. Graham says.

Scott looks worried. "Can I still be treasurer if I have a C in math?"

"In that case, I'll run too." Brittney raises her hand.

There goes my last chance to run unopposed.

Sticker Girl is officially running for president.

Tommy catches up to me on our way out of class. "Good luck," he says. "You'll need it."

So this is what happens when I finally stick my head out of my shell? Why did I think it was a good idea to run for student council? I was obviously NOT thinking.

After class, Bev appoints herself my official campaign manager. "This is going to be great—right, Craig?" she asks her new cupcake friend.

"You said it!" Craig answers.

Worst. Idea. Ever.

I'm sunk.

something I'm good At

Since Ms. Graham is so big on teaching us about the election process, we'll use the week before the election to run actual political campaigns. Bev thinks we should have a party and have my dad make some of his famous churros with chocolate, cinnamon, and chilies, but I have something else in mind.

One of the benefits of being shy is that you can get really good at listening. I've been in so many situations where I had no idea what to say to people—not just grownups, but other kids too—so I learned how to observe and listen. I can use those skills now to find out what issues the other kids in my class are concerned with. Just thinking about approaching kids I don't know and asking for their opinions is scary, but it makes more sense than offering kids a balloon or lollipop with my name attached to the stick.

Recess has never been a favorite time for me—I usually spend it reading or playing with stickers—but it's the best time to talk to other kids. I don't want to look like a nerd, so I don't take notes, but let me say for the record that I WANT to.

When I ask Craig if he's up for hiding in my bag and writing down responses, he says yes. "But then," he says, "cupcakes are terrible at spelling."

I take a deep breath and go over to Hilary and Kim at the climbing structure. Here goes. "Hi! I was just wondering if there are any issues that are important to you in this election."

Kim gives me a strange look. "Aren't you just supposed to give us food?"

I tell her I will definitely have food at the rally later this week but right now I want to see if they can suggest any improvements for our class.

"Bigger cubbies," Hilary says. "Ours are old and too small."

I hope Craig is taking good notes from inside my bag. I thank Hilary and Kim for their input.

It takes more courage than I usually have to interrupt Jake, Chad, and Danny's game of alien tag, but when they finally stop running they also have some ideas to share.

"We don't take enough field trips," Chad says.

Danny and Jake agree.

At my last school, I *loved* going on field trips. Getting out of the classroom was always a treat, and I liked seeing how my classmates acted out in the real world, not just behind their desks. Maybe taking field trips with my *new* class would help me figure out how to fit in better with them.

By the time we go back inside for math, I've gotten a real feel for what everyone cares about in this election. I lock myself in the girls' bathroom and look at Craig's notes.

"*Feeld tripp?*" I ask. "Really?"

Craig shrugs. "I told you cupcakes can't spell."

When I head back to class, Bev almost knocks me over. "Where have you been? We've got to finish making plans for the rally." She leans in close and tells me she just heard Caitlyn is bringing fortune cookies with little slips of paper inside that read VOTE FOR CAITLYN.

I guess if you're someone like Bev or Caitlyn

who's comfortable with herself, you don't need to overprepare. Bev might be worried about finding the perfect entertainment or food for the rally, but all I can focus on is going over Craig's mangled notes and putting together my ideas.

I have
to give a
speech!!!

on the campaign trail

At dinner, my brother Eric starts in as soon as he hears I'm running. "President of what?" he asks. "The wallflower club? You better hope one of your friends' pet rocks doesn't run against you."

My mom tells him to keep quiet, but he's not saying anything I haven't already thought myself.

"I think it's great," Mom continues. "You have good organizational skills—you'll be a real asset to the student council."

Dad shoots Eric a look that shuts him up before he can begin a new insult.

James is in his booster seat, trying to eat with a spoon. There's so much rice on the floor, it looks like outside the church at my cousin Sofia's wedding.

After dinner, I head to my room to try to come up with a campaign strategy. Of course, it's hard to get anything done with Craig constantly throwing his two cents in.

"I just thought it would be more challenging for you to run *against* somebody," Craig says.

I try to explain that not having someone to run against was exactly *why* I wanted to run for secretary. "I wasn't looking for a challenge."

"You should throw a big party," Craig says with gusto. "Every candidate has one."

He doesn't need to tell me that I have to plan *some* kind of party; Bev says it's a tradition. I'll bet anything Tommy and Caitlyn aren't one bit worried, and here I am a nervous wreck. Could any of my new stickers help?

I find the magic sheet right where I left it—in the bottom drawer of my desk with the thank-you cards I send when relatives give me presents. I look at the stickers—maybe I can use the pizza sticker for a party? Or how about the palette of paint—every campaign needs posters!

I run to my closet and find the poster for the volcano project I did a few months ago. I flip it over and stare at the blank sheet. Will the paint palette be magical? There's only one way to find out.

whoosh! poof! Bam!

The palette

fits perfectly in my hand; I pick up the brush carefully. Do I use this like regular poster paint?

"Don't look at me," Craig says. "I was clueless about the treasure chest, remember?"

I dip the brush into the circle of turquoise paint. It feels strange to write the words VOTE FOR MARTINA, but if I'm running for student council, voting for me is exactly what I need to persuade people to do. (Tommy probably won't even make posters. He'll just tell a few jokes and end up winning in a landslide. Caitlyn's posters will, of course, be perfectly lettered, the way her home-work always is.)

Usually I can barely draw a tree—they all come out looking like lollipops wearing clown wigs—but today my art skills are AMAZING. Stars, balloons, rockets all flow from my brush. The lettering is fluid and perfectly spaced;

the wet paint glistens the most gorgeous blue I've ever seen.

When I show the poster to Craig, his eyes spin around in circles. "Must vote for Martina," he says. "Must vote for Martina."

It's almost as if he's spellbound by the words on the poster. I snap my fingers in front of Craig's tiny face.

"Must vote for Martina."

Is this *hypnotizing* paint?!

"I'm kidding!" Craig says. "But I have to admit that poster is beautiful."

Bev has to see this! With these results, we SHOULD have a POSTER PARTY! But she's stuck running errands with her dad and there's no way to show her a picture.

I keep telling my parents I need to have a cell phone. They say I'm responsible enough but still too young. *Hel-lo!* Time is of the essence! I've got a presidential campaign to plan and I don't have a way to reach my campaign manager!

Or do I?

I look at the sheet of magic stickers. Maybe I can use the cell phone to text Bev a picture of my poster. I don't usually like to use two stickers in one day, but running for class president is important.

Whoosh! POOF! BAM!

The

cell Phone

sticker comes to life in my hand; it's shiny and sparkly, in a rainbow case. The screen is full of colorful apps of the very latest games. This phone looks like it does everything!

Except take photos.

And send texts.

And have a dial tone.

I hit the SEND button several times but nothing happens. None of the apps work either. Am I supposed to hook up to some special magical network to use this phone? This is what I get for using two stickers in one day.

I'm a terrible Sticker Girl!

surprise party

I don't need Craig to remind me that using magical poster paint *might* be considered cheating, but Bev thinks it's the greatest idea on the planet.

"Candidates use whatever tools they have," she tells me in school the next day. "If that paint is as good as you say, you'll have the best posters in the history of student council campaigns!"

I tell Bev I just want to be fair to Tommy and Caitlyn.

Bev holds up her hand like she's taking a vow.

"I promise to run a hundred percent clean campaign. But if we take advantage of a little magic along the way, is that so wrong?"

I end up agreeing with her—we *should* use the magic paint. Not only do I have to give a speech in a few days, I have a social studies test to worry about. At this point, I'll take all the help I can get.

Later, when I get home from school after barely passing my test, I find that Eric is working with Dad at the diner so at least he won't be here to disrupt the poster party. I'm still worried no one will show up, but Bev insists she's got it covered.

I thought of peeling off the pizza sticker for the party, but Dad dropped off trays full of nachos, so I'll save the sticker for another time. I take out several jars of poster paint I find in the garage.

"No way," Bev says. "We need these posters to be amazing—everyone should use the magic paint."

"But won't people think it's weird if we all use the same palette?"

"You can say you're trying not to be wasteful or that these are your favorite colors," Bev says. "Besides, everyone just wants to have fun—they're not going to ask a million questions."

I hope she's right. It's not only the palette that's making me feel anxious, it's being the center of attention. Yes, Bev is my campaign manager and she's friendly with most of our classmates, but what if kids show up and I have nothing to say? Suppose I ask them to make posters and then just stand there, unable to find words? I know most people would think having a group of classmates come over to help and support you would be a *good* thing, so why do I feel so nervous and afraid?

It's as if Mom can read my mind, because she comes over and pulls me into a hug. "Even if it's just you, Bev, and me who show up, we'll have a great time."

But it's not just the three of us. More than half my class arrives at four on the dot (even Samantha and Jillian, who I've never even spoken to). I put on music while Bev hands out poster board and some bottles of glitter she brought from home. Between the nachos, the glitter, and so many of my classmates being here, it's a real party and no one seems to mind sharing one palette of paint.

I just hope the magic comes through—and it does! My palette gives everyone incredible artistic abilities. None of my classmates can believe how well they can suddenly paint.

"I'm a whiz today!" Jillian says. "Most of the time I can't even draw a straight line."

Bev's posters are all in gorgeous, glittery cursive. Samantha even wishes she had someone to run against for secretary so she could make campaign posters too.

I keep checking the palette to see if any of the paints are close to running out, but the palette is endlessly full of the deepest, most vibrant colors I've ever seen.

When I go to my room to get more poster board, I spot the fake table hiding the treasure chest and get an idea. I come back to the dining room table with a shoebox full of jewels.

"These look so real!" Samantha says.

"I know." Bev smirks. "We thought so too."

The jewels and glitter we glue onto the posters make the glistening paint look even better. And Jillian's poster of me standing at a podium looks as if it was made by a professional.

"Oh my!" Mom examines the colorful posters leaning against the wall. "Each one is more gorgeous than the next!"

Some of the slogans are embarrassing and make me feel like if I win, I'll have a lot to live up to. Bev's FLY HIGH WITH MARTINA *is* kind of funny, especially with the three lifelike figures she drew riding a Pegasus in the sky. I also like Samantha's drawing of a koala in a tree with the caption "Martina is Koalafied for President!"

When Chad asks what I'm going to talk about in my speech, I tell him he actually gave me one of the main ideas in my platform. "I liked your idea about taking more field trips," I explain. "I think I'll talk about that."

He seems happy his idea was good enough to share, and I wonder if maybe next time he'll run for student council too.

As everyone takes a break to eat, I look through the posters my classmates made. Do they really think all these nice things about me?

Bev shoves a handful of nachos into her mouth.

"All we have to do is hang these masterpieces outside the classroom and you're a shoo-in!"

Even though the poster party was supposed to end before dinner, there's so much food, most of my classmates are full by the time their parents pick them up.

After the posters are dry, Mom helps me carefully stack them to take to school tomorrow.

"You've made some nice friends here." She points to the beautiful flowers and ponies on one of the posters. "Artistic too."

I don't tell her *I'm* the one who painted the poster she's talking about. She *knows* I've never drawn anything so perfectly proportioned in my life, and I don't feel like explaining the power of the magical palette.

I give Mom a hug and head back to my room, feeling a bit overwhelmed.

Halfway through diving onto my bed, I realize I'm about to land on Craig and roll out of the way. When he asks how the party went, I tell him it was great—but tiring.

"It's hard for you, isn't it?" Craig asks. "Having to talk to so many people at the same time."

"Is it that obvious?" I stare at the ceiling. "I've never been much of a party person."

"It gets easier the more you do it," Craig says. "At least that's what I've heard."

I close my eyes, take a deep breath, and hope he's right.

Presto, Change-o

The next morning, I'm exhausted but happy. I don't know if this is what it feels like to be popular, but if it is, it's pretty good.

"What are you so happy about?" Eric says, shoving a piece of toast with peanut butter into his mouth as he talks. I make sure no crumbs fall into the trunk of Mom's car, where I've neatly placed all the posters.

Eric checks out the colorful posters. He'll never admit it, but I can tell he's impressed.

And when Ms. Graham sees Bev and me hanging them up in the hall before class, she's awestruck too.

"Martina, these are gorgeous!" She waves her cast in the air and calls over Mr. Tavares and Mrs. Lynch, who also gush.

I tell Bev the paint palette might be the best magic sticker I've ever had.

Bev fastens the last poster to the tiled wall, then puts her hands on her hips. "You rode a *Pegasus*, remember? It doesn't get any better than that."

Deidre and Abby walk by but stop when they see the posters. They both smile and Abby gives us a thumbs-up.

"Martina, you might actually *win* this!" Bev says.

I hope she's right, but Tommy and Caitlyn made posters last night too. They might not be as lifelike and colorful as mine, but they're still good. I especially like the collage Caitlyn made with photos of everyone in our class.

It's hard to concentrate in Language Arts when there's so much buzz about the election. Usually when there's a fair or show during school, I'm on the outskirts of all the activity. It feels weird to be in the *middle* of things this time. I wish I knew how other kids get work done with all these distractions, because I can barely listen to today's discussion on nouns and verbs.

Back in the hall after class, there's even more commotion—but for a different reason this time. Kids are whispering and pointing to the walls covered with posters. My beautiful posters are now completely blank.

Some of the edges still have glitter and glued-on jewels, but all the lettering and amazing drawings my classmates painted are gone.

"How did this happen?" Bev whispers. "Was that disappearing paint?"

If I wasn't supposed to use that palette, why did it come alive?

Tommy and a few of his friends hurry over.

"Knock-knock," Tommy says.

Bev and I ignore him until I realize he's not going away.

"Who's there?" I ask.

"Not your posters!" Tommy and his friends laugh. Bev and I do not.

"It's actually kind of cool," Tommy continues. "I wish the grades on my report card could disappear before I brought it home."

Caitlyn comes over wearing an exaggerated frown and tells me she's sorry. I can't decide if she really means it or not.

It's hard to believe an hour ago I was one of the happiest kids on the planet. Now all the work

my friends and I did was for nothing. Bev hands me a marker and we frantically write VOTE FOR MARTINA on a few of the empty sheets of poster board, but they look hasty and scrawled compared with the other candidates' posters.

I tell myself, *Don't cry. Don't cry. Don't cry.* But I want to.

Eileen

"It could be worse," Bev says, trying to cheer me up at home later.

"It's like you're a magician and you made the paint disappear," Craig says.

"I wish I could make MYSELF disappear," I answer.

"Maybe one of these will lift your spirits." Bev goes to my desk drawer and waves the sheet of magic stickers in front of me. "It's a perfect day to ride in a hot-air balloon."

"With my luck, it would probably pop on somebody's satellite dish."

But Bev's not giving up. "Hey, *she* looks cool!" Bev points to the sticker of the girl playing soccer. "I think a nice game of soccer is just the thing to take your mind off your speech."

I have to admit, I'm a little curious. I've never had a *human* sticker before, and the girl on the sheet looks about our age.

"Let's see if she's any good," I say. "But we'd better go outside to peel her off in case she keeps running."

Bev and I hurry to my backyard, and then I close my eyes and gently peel off the sticker.

whoosh! POOf! Bam!
Girl Soccer player

Suddenly there are *three* of us in my backyard. The new girl yells, "Heads up!" and kicks the ball hard. It sails through the small space between Bev and me.

"Whoa!" Bev says. "That's some aim!"

The girl runs over and scoops up the ball. She holds it in front of herself and gets ready to kick it again.

Bev and I watch in wonder as the ball sails into the basketball net attached to the garage.

"That's amazing!" I run over to see the girl who used to be a sticker. Her wavy red hair is pulled back in a ponytail. She's wearing shorts and a nylon top that says O'CONNELL across the back.

"Eileen O'Connell," she says. "Nice to meet you."

Bev and I introduce ourselves and ask if we can play. I run inside to put on sneakers, but by the time I come back out Eileen and Bev are nowhere to be found.

"Over here!" Bev shouts.

It takes a few seconds for me to see the two of them halfway up the sycamore tree on the front lawn. My family's lived here for a year, but I've never had the courage to try to climb it.

"Come on up!" Eileen calls.

I fake enthusiasm and tell them I would, but I'm dying to play soccer. They jump out of the tree with no hesitation at all.

I'm an okay soccer player but I can't match Bev, who plays on a travel team. With the diner open every weekend, I never felt comfortable asking my parents to take me to all those games.

As expected, Eileen is a marvel, running across the yard twice as fast as either Bev or me.

Bev shoots me a look of surprise and joy that makes me run even faster to keep up. When Mom takes out the recycling, she watches us play and I know I'll have to introduce her to Eileen.

I've practiced trying to explain the magical stickers to my parents, but explaining a talking cupcake—never mind a living, breathing soccer player—sounds ridiculous and I always decide not to.

"Mom, this is Eileen. She's new in town." (Technically true.)

Mom tells Eileen she's quite the soccer player.

"I've been playing forever," Eileen says. (Possibly also true.)

Her comment leaves me wondering about the stickers' lives when they're not with me. Craig never gives me any details; maybe Eileen will be more helpful.

Bev runs to the opposite end of the yard with the ball. "Thanks for leaving your goal wide open!" Eileen darts off to stop her and I try to formulate a plan. Should I ask Mom if Eileen can sleep over? Should I hide Eileen in my room? I have no idea what to do with a *human* sticker.

Turns out I don't need to worry, because Eileen walks over holding the ball with Bev right behind her. "Bev and I are heading out," Eileen says.

I just stare at her. What is she talking about?

"I'm going to stay at Bev's," Eileen continues. "She says there's plenty of room." I look over at Bev, who shrugs and looks down at her sneakers.

When Ms. Henley from next door comes over to talk to Mom, I pull Bev aside.

"Don't you think Eileen should stay at my house with the other stickers?" But what I'm really wondering is why Eileen wants to leave. She's MY sticker, not Bev's!

"I felt weird when she asked if she could come over," Bev explains. "But I didn't know how to say no."

"You just say no." I lower my voice so my mom doesn't get suspicious. "But if you want her to stay with you, it's fine with me."

Bev looks at me again to make sure.

"We'll see you tomorrow, okay?" Eileen comes over and balances the ball on her foot before she kicks it down the street and runs after it. Finally, Bev takes off after her.

Mom finishes her conversation with Ms. Henley and walks back over. We watch the girls head down the street.

"You okay?" Mom asks.

I nod as if it's no big deal, but it is. And I don't know which is worse—that my best friend just left me for a sticker or that my sticker just left me for my best friend.

DO I HaVE to?

The next day, Bev's dad gives us a ride to school. When I climb in, I'm shocked to see Eileen in the car.

We talk about the election until Bev's dad takes a call on his headset. Bev spins around in her seat with a huge grin. "I told Mom that Eileen's visiting her grandmother to see if she should transfer to our school," she whispers. "I asked if she could call the school and get Eileen a visitor's pass for the day so Eileen can check it out."

"Your school sounds great," Eileen says.

Eileen is no longer wearing her soccer uniform but a Star Wars T-shirt and a pair of Bev's jeans—her favorite pair.

A million thoughts flood my head: How does Bev always convince her mom to help with her crazy stunts? Will Eileen get into trouble at school that I'LL end up getting blamed for? And most important—EILEEN IS A STICKER!

I don't have time to argue, because Bev immediately starts in about today's rally. I take out the notes for my speech, but she grabs them from my hands.

"You've been over your speech a hundred times," Bev says. "We have to talk about entertainment!"

I tell her that at my last school, rallies were about handing out flyers and talking to candidates.

"Sounds boring," Eileen says.

"You've never even BEEN to school," I say. "How would you know?"

"I just think we should be prepared in case Tommy and Caitlyn bring more than speeches." Bev hands me back my notes. She asks if I brought my sheet of stickers.

It feels weird talking about the magic stickers in front of Eileen, who less than twenty-four hours ago was a sticker herself. I tell Bev that of course I have them.

"We might need to break out the pizza to compete with Caitlyn's fortune cookies."

"I've always wanted to try pizza!" Eileen pipes up.

Eileen's boundless enthusiasm is officially getting on my nerves.

When Eileen signs in at the main office, she's so excited you'd think she was just given a Lifetime Achievement award instead of a standard visitor's pass. In class, Ms. Graham lets her sit next to Bev, since Danny is out sick.

Ms. Graham discusses the last presidential election and what makes a good campaign. The whole time she talks, I read through the notes for my speech. How are these other kids paying attention? I'm too nervous to talk about Democrats and Republicans!

"All right, enough theory," Ms. Graham says. "Let's head to the cafeteria and see some politics in action!"

Everyone hurries out, but I'm glued to my seat. I know I have to, but I don't want to move. Bev literally has to pull me out of the chair to join the rest of the class.

Ms. Graham reprimands Billy and Lisa for

fidgeting during Samantha's speech. She's still running unopposed, so she'll definitely win. Why did Craig and Bev have to interfere with my foolproof plan?

"Thank you, Samantha," Ms. Graham says. "Now we'll hear from our first candidate for president, Martina Rivera." Ms. Graham hands me the mic, and Bev gives me a little shove and a smile.

I close my eyes and tell myself that even if I lose the election, at least I tried and that's WAY more than I've ever done before so I should be proud of myself. That makes me feel a tiny bit better, but not much.

I have no choice but to begin. "I'm Martina Rivera and I'm running for class president." I have my speech memorized but still use the index cards like a security blanket.

"The number one thing I will focus on as class president is to make sure we take lots of field trips this year." I see a few kids look up;

I might have their attention. "We have money left over from the outing at Griffith Observatory, and we can all agree *that* trip was a success."

A few kids murmur in agreement.

"If—I mean *when*—I'm elected president I'll fight for us to do lots of learning *outside* the classroom too."

Basing my whole campaign platform on class trips might not be the smartest choice, but talking about my organizational skills the way my parents suggested felt like bragging. And I certainly can't list any leadership abilities, mostly because I've always made sure to hide in the back of any line, not be in the front.

When I finish my speech, Bev bangs on the floor with her fists, trying to invite the others into her *"Mar-ti-na"* chant, but it doesn't catch on. I slip in next to her and wait for Tommy to take the stage.

"Okay, guys—here's what I'M going to do if elected." Tommy stretches his arms in front of him and cracks his knuckles. "We're going to start having FUN around here—every day of the week!"

He's barely begun, but some kids are already cheering.

"When I'm class president, Monday will officially be known as Monkey Business Monday! Followed by Toga Tuesdays, Wacky Wednesdays, Throw-up Thursdays, and Food Fight Fridays!"

The class is so riled up, Ms. Graham has to tell everyone to calm down.

"No one takes him seriously," Bev whispers. "He'll never do any of those things!"

"Tommy seems like so much fun!" Eileen says. "He gets *my* vote."

My jaw almost drops to the floor. My own sticker isn't going to vote for me!

Bev just laughs. "I guess Ms. Graham is right and every vote DOES have to be earned."

His campaign may be ludicrous, but Tommy's just shown he's a hundred times wackier than I am, and that's what most kids will remember. (That and my nonexistent posters.)

Caitlyn is next. She brings a third-grade girl to play "Hail to the Chief" on a recorder as she approaches the podium.

"My fellow classmates," she begins, looking each student in the eye. "You deserve a president who understands and will fight tirelessly to represent you and bring about the changes this school desperately needs."

Caitlyn's not even holding any index cards. I don't stand a chance. When she finishes her speech, everyone applauds—Ms. Graham most of all.

I barely pay attention to Mike's and Tanya's speeches for vice president, or Scott's and Brittney's reasons why they should be elected treasurer. At the end of the speeches, Ms. Graham tells us to use the rest of the time to campaign.

"Let the rally begin!" Tommy shouts.

While his friends hand out flyers, Tommy takes three cartons of chocolate milk from behind the lunch counter and starts juggling.

Caitlyn and her friends pass out fortune cookies and hand out props for kids to hold while they pose in Caitlyn's makeshift photo booth.

Bev looks at me with an I-told-you-so face.

"This isn't campaigning!" I say.

"Sure it is. You just didn't want to hear it." Bev looks upset, and I wonder if it's because I'm going to lose or because I didn't take her advice.

Eileen approaches and hands us both flyers.

"Tommy for president!"

Bev and I swipe the stack of flyers from her hand.

"He asked me to help," Eileen says. "Should I have said no? I thought he was your friend."

Bev hardly ever loses her cool, but she looks like she's about to. "Martina, what are we going to do?"

A smile creeps across Bev's face as I take out the sheet of stickers from my bag. Pizza? Hot-air balloon?

We both stare at the zombie DJ.

Bev reaches for my hand as it hovers over the sticker. "You do realize this could backfire, right? Maybe he's a DJ, but maybe he'll eat people's brains too."

I tell Bev at this point I'm willing to risk it. "Let's just hope he focuses more on the music than on eating our classmates."

I wrinkle my nose and lift up the edge of the sticker.

whoosh! poof! Bam!

I hope I didn't just make the biggest mistake of my life.

zombie BOY

The **zombie**

with the headphones and laptop lurches to life beside me. Mike comes running over. "Did you get this guy at the same place you rented the animatronic Pegasus?" he asks.

The zombie grunts and belches in Mike's face.

"Whoa!" Mike laughs. "Sorry—didn't know you were real. Nice makeup, dude!"

The zombie adjusts his headphones, then opens his laptop and rapidly hits the keyboard. Sound suddenly fills the cafeteria.

The music is unlike anything I've ever heard; it's fast and hypnotic and gets everyone in the class on their feet.

"Hey!" Tommy calls. "Who wants to see me juggle FOUR cartons of milk?" But people can't take their eyes off the zombie, who moves rapidly from song to song.

"That beat is awesome!" Samantha turns to me. "Where did you find this guy?"

Bev beats me to the punch, explaining that I hired a local DJ complete with costume and makeup for today's rally.

"To make up for your blank posters?" Tommy's

usually pretty nice, so I'm not sure this election is bringing out the best in him.

The zombie is the same size as I am and I suddenly wonder if he's our age. Suppose he's two thousand years old? Did he go to school when he was alive? And most important, can he help me win this election?

The zombie tilts his head back and lets out a shattering noise that quiets us in an instant. Then he turns up the volume and starts playing our school anthem. How does he even know it? My classmates clap and sing along.

I freeze when I spot Ms. Graham in the corner of the cafeteria. I'm about to repeat the rent-a-DJ story, but I don't have to.

"Martina, you are full of surprises," she says. "Music is EXACTLY what this rally needed. Great school spirit!"

Before I can say anything, Ms. Graham is in a dance line behind the zombie, holding her cast above her head as she and the others weave through the room. Is it safe to conga with a zombie?

Everyone seems to be having fun, except for Tommy and Caitlyn.

"*Mar-ti-na! Mar-ti-na!*" Bev chants.

This time it catches on. Soon the whole room is chanting with her.

"Great rally!" Samantha says.

As soon as she turns away, Craig pops out of my bag. "You have to admit, this is much better than running unopposed." He motions to the zombie. "I had no idea someone with so many dangling body parts could have such a good ear."

"I'm not sure he HAS both ears."

When the song ends, Ms. Graham covers her mouth with her hands like a megaphone: "Everybody back to class!"

No one wants to go; we're all having too much fun.

"It's time to vote!" Ms. Graham continues.

How am I supposed to go to class when I've just unleashed a zombie? It's not like I can shove him in a locker—everybody thinks he's a real kid! I finally remember there's an out-of-order stall in the girls' bathroom. If I hide him there, will he stay put?

After making sure no one's around, Bev, Eileen, and I guide Zombie Boy into the broken stall.

He tries to drink out of the toilet.

I spin him back around and lead him to the janitor's closet.

"Suppose he starts playing music again?" Eileen asks.

I slide the zombie's laptop out of his hands; he grunts unhappily.

"We have to find something to keep him busy," Bev says.

We rummage through the closet until I find something that might amuse him: a roll of toilet paper. "Hopefully this'll keep him occupied till we come back."

The three of us hurry to class. We race to our seats as Ms. Graham passes out ballots.

Eileen asks Ms. Graham if she can vote too, but Ms. Graham says no. Considering how much Eileen was just helping Tommy, I'm not sure it's a bad thing she can't.

Tommy high-fives and fist-bumps the kids on either side of him. I doubt anyone in our class took Tommy's campaign platform seriously, but kids know what they're getting with Tommy—a goofy comic who likes to have fun. I've been so quiet since I transferred to this school that most of my classmates don't know me well enough to give me a second thought. Even with Bev as my campaign manager, there's only so much of her popularity that can rub off on me. And Caitlyn's speech was really good—even *I* want to vote for her. But I know I can't.

As strange as it feels to cast a vote for myself, I do. Ms. Graham collects all the slips of paper and tells us to do some silent reading while she counts the ballots. As if I can concentrate on reading! Fifteen minutes later, she walks around to lean on the front of her desk and faces the class.

"It's time to hear the results of your foray into the democratic process." She clears her throat. "Our new student council secretary is Samantha Phillips."

Everyone applauds. All I'm thinking is, that could've been me, winning with no opponent!

Samantha holds her hands in front of her mouth as if she's shocked, which is cute but kind of obnoxious at the same time.

"Our new class treasurer is Scott Palermo."

Scott did have some great posters. He seems thrilled to be treasurer—even though most of the time he still counts on his fingers.

"Mike Belmont will be our new vice president," Ms. Graham continues.

I'm happy for Mike. He's always been one of my favorite kids in class, even before we were friends.

"And the president of our class this year will be . . . drumroll, please."

Tommy interrupts. "Aww, man! I can't believe I lost to a kid named Drumroll Please! He didn't even give a speech!"

Leave it to Tommy to get in one more joke before the announcement.

Ms. Graham smiles. "Martina Rivera."

WHAT?! Is this happening or is this some kind of alternate reality, like my stickers? Did Ms. Graham just say my name? How could Tommy and Caitlyn have lost to *me*?

Kids are turned around in their seats, applauding and smiling. It's a good thing no one asks for a speech because my throat feels locked; I doubt I could squeeze out a word if I tried.

Bev jumps up and down in her seat, and when the bell rings she almost knocks me over.

"I *told* you," she says. "Kids want to do things like go on field trips, not have food fights! And that zombie DJ at the rally was killer!"

Caitlyn is one of the first to congratulate me. I tell her she ran a great campaign. Tommy looks shocked that he lost. Eileen gives me a big hug.

I'm embarrassed by all the attention and luckily have an excuse to hurry out of class—I've got to get Zombie Boy out of the custodian's closet. When I open the closet door, I can barely see him underneath all the toilet paper, which is now strewn everywhere. I pull him out and close the door just as the custodian turns the corner toward us.

Where am I going to hide a zombie?

The DJ boy trails toilet paper behind him all the way home. I pick it up as it falls and try

to make sense of today. Whether it was the zombie's great music, the issues, or that Caitlyn and Tommy split the vote, I don't know—but somehow I'm the new president of our class.

It doesn't seem real—but neither does walking home from school with a zombie.

This is my life!

I am

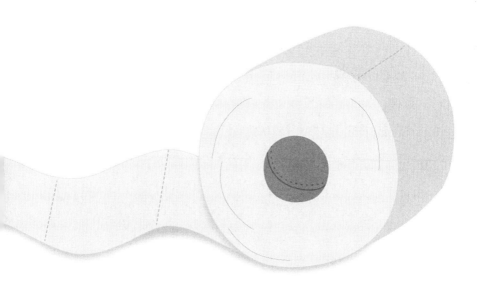

The After-party

Bev and Eileen insist on coming over to celebrate. Bev wants Zombie Boy to DJ again so we can dance in my room, but I need to figure out where he's going to stay. Both my parents park in the driveway, so there's room in the garage. The weather's been warm and the zombie will probably be fine. (Unless zombies are SUPPOSED to be cold.) We fill a cooler full of apples, juice boxes, and potato chips and pile up blankets in the corner of the garage behind the Halloween decorations.

When Eric was my age, he was obsessed with Halloween and spent hours filling the yard with Styrofoam tombstones and plastic bones. Now that he's in high school, the only thing he wants to do on Halloween is hang out with his friends and scare younger kids. I make sure the coast is clear, then lead Zombie Boy to the makeshift cemetery in our garage.

"Look, all your buddies are here." Bev gestures to the Frankenstein and vampire statues that light up the lawn in October. He seems right at home with the graveyard gear, but his face really brightens when I give him back his laptop.

"Who knew zombies were such nerds?" Bev says.

I close the garage door and head inside.

Back in my room, Bev and Eileen start jumping around. "You won the election! We have to celebrate!"

I DO want to celebrate, but I also wonder if it was ethical to use my stickers in the campaign.

I ask Eileen and Bev if they think I won fair and square.

"Yes, but if you're not sure, there's only one thing you can do about it now," Bev says. "And that's be the best class president you can be."

She's right, and that's exactly what I plan to do.

Eileen sees the sheet of magic stickers poking out from my bag. She traces the outline of herself with her finger. "How does it work?" she asks. "Do you have to do anything special when you peel us off?"

I explain about the poof of confetti and the noise.

"I don't remember that," Eileen says.

I ask her if it feels like

she's sleeping when she's on the sheet of stickers.

Eileen closes her eyes. "It's quiet." She takes one of my bracelets from the nightstand and tries it on. "It's much more fun here."

For the first time since Eileen's been with us, I feel like she's my friend as much as Bev's. But I don't ask where she's staying tonight, in case she decides to crash at Bev's again.

Eileen points to the chipmunk ballerina on the magic sheet, and I can tell she's curious to see what the process looks like. I feel kind of weird letting loose a rodent, especially since I just hid a zombie in our garage.

"Come on," Bev says. "You just won an election—why not?"

With the two of them egging me on, I peel off the second sticker of the day.

whoosh! POOF! Bam!

A chipmunk

in a tiara and a pink tutu pirouettes across my bed,
faster than I've ever
seen anyone dance
before. The tiny crea-
ture leaps over the
pillows so quickly
that I have to duck.
Lily barks, unsure
what she's barking at.
Eileen, Bev, and I squeal with
delight.

The brown blur in pink ballet slippers spins
across my nightstand faster than a top in a tor-
nado. The chipmunk comes to an unexpected
halt and bows deeply before me.

"That was amazing!" I hold out my hand and

the ballerina leaps into it, landing perfectly. "And what is your name?"

"Walter," the ballerina says. "And I love to dance!"

Family Night

Surely the opportunity to hang out with a chatty male chipmunk ballerina would be enough to persuade Eileen to stay over, but when Bev's mom comes to pick her up a few minutes later, Eileen sheepishly asks if she can go too. I can tell by Bev's eyes that this is awkward, so I immediately tell Eileen it's fine.

Craig, of course, can't help but comment. "I think it's strange that Eileen's at Bev's again. I mean, what's wrong with *us*?"

It's a question I'd been asking myself too. I

hope I didn't just win an election only to lose a best friend.

My parents are thrilled that I won and insist on inviting our extended family to the diner this weekend to celebrate my victory.

My cousins Beth and Lucia are excited that I'm the new class president and make me tell them all about the campaign. Eric and my older cousins set up goals in the parking lot and play soccer while my aunts bring out food from the kitchen and my uncles tell stories and talk about sports.

Beth and Lucia would *love* to meet Craig and Walter, but I would have opened myself up to too many questions if I showed them to Beth and Lucia. Before everyone arrived, I hid both of them in the back room behind a giant bag of potatoes, where they could enjoy the party without being seen. I did think about taking Zombie Boy, but since there's electricity and Wi-Fi in the garage, he chose to binge-watch old episodes of *The Walking Dead* instead.

In the back room of the diner, Craig pulls me aside. "Don't leave me alone with Walter—I'm afraid he might try to eat me."

"Please!" Walter says. "In the history of the world, have you ever seen a ballet dancer eat a cupcake? Have you?"

I tell Craig that Walter does have a point, but to reassure him, I slip my cupcake friend back into his plastic container. Walter finds a corner of the storage room to practice, then laces his pointe shoes.

I *can* share *one* of the stickers with my cousins—the treasure chest. Before leaving the house, I filled my backpack with the beautiful— but fake—gems, which I now empty onto the table of our booth. Beth and Lucia love the jewels, and we line them up along the tabletop in different patterns, like a gemstone quilt.

"Now that's the kind of table I need in my house!"

The three of us jump out of the booth to hug

our abuelita, who's just arrived with a group of friends. I'm still not sure if she had anything to do with my magic sticker sheets, and every time I ask her, she changes the subject or just smiles.

"Congratulations, Marti," she says when she kisses me. "You'll make a wonderful class president."

"Well, I *did* have some help." I raise my eyebrows to see if she gets the hint about my magical stickers, but she doesn't take the bait.

"I heard you had lots of friends making

posters," she continues. "Posters always help in an election."

Does she know about the palette sticker? Does she know the paint was magical—until it disappeared?

Beth and Lucia lead our grandmother over to Dad, who twirls her in the middle of the diner as if they're dancing. It doesn't take long before everyone starts dancing for real.

When Bev invited my class to a party at the diner earlier this year, she told me afterward how surprised she was by how fun-loving my family is. I know she meant it as a compliment, but I also know she was taken aback because when people first meet me, *fun-loving* probably isn't the phrase that comes to mind. Hanging out with Bev has certainly been nice; I just hope it's been that way for her too.

There's suddenly a commotion—it turns out Mom's trying to pry some jewels out of James's mouth. After removing a few drooly sapphires, she shoots me a stern look to put the jewels away.

In between helping with the food—and accepting congratulations from my relatives—I check up on Craig in the storage room.

"I HATE not being invited to parties," he complains.

"You're here, aren't you? I could've left you at home." I look around the room. "Is Walter still rehearsing?"

Craig shakes his head and tells me Walter took off a while ago.

That's when I hear my aunt Carmen scream.

"Rata!"

I run into the front room to find Dad swinging a broom and my abuelita trying to calm down my aunt. When a pink blur passes through my legs, I realize it's Walter. I'm immediately concerned for his safety, but when I catch up to him back in the storage room he's exhilarated.

"That's the best cardio workout I've had in ages," he says. "I can feel the adrenaline racing through my whole body."

I scoop up the chipmunk and hide him behind

several large jars of olives.

"I *hate* olives," Walter says. "They're so fatty—get them away!"

"This is no time to be fussy," I whisper. "Thanks to you, everyone thinks Dad's restaurant has rats!"

"RATS?!" Walter screams. "Rats are *terrible* dancers! Have you ever seen a rat do an arabesque? It's *embarrassing!*"

Of course Eric has to get into the act—he and my cousins Otto and Jorge race into the storage room to find the rodent that's crashing our family party. I lean against the shelf, blocking not only Walter but Craig.

"Get out of the way, Martina," Eric shouts.

"If there was a rat, it's gone by now," I say.

Otto stops in his tracks. "Are you calling my mother a liar? If she says there was a rat, there was a rat!"

I apologize to my cousin, basically so the three boys will leave. When they finally do, I shove Walter and Craig into my bag.

"There's not enough oxygen," Walter complains. "My muscles will tense up."

These stickers can be *so* high maintenance.

"Just stay put until we eat," I say. "Then we can go home."

I remind myself that this party was supposed to be for *me*. Is it asking too much to have a little fun tonight? Especially since my best friend seems to be spending all her time with one of my stickers?

When I get back to the counter, my aunt has

calmed down and the fuss is pretty much over—although Dad is still telling anyone who'll listen that his diner does *not* have rats.

My abuelita raises her glass in a toast. "To Marti—may she be a fair and compassionate president."

My grandmother obviously thinks my new post on the student council is *way* more important than it is, but my relatives lift their glasses anyway. We pass around platters of food; because I'm sitting next to James in his booster seat, I serve him a little from every dish.

Since I'm wedged into one of the circular booths with James and several of my cousins, checking on Walter and Craig in my bag on the floor is nearly impossible. When I can finally duck underneath the table, I find Walter sitting on the floor scooping up rice with his tiny chipmunk hands.

"Your brother is a *slob*. Did any of this arroz con pollo end up in his mouth?" Walter licks his tiny fingers. "I know it's mostly carbs, but it's *delicious.*"

Luckily, there's so much commotion that no one hears Walter—except maybe Eric, who suddenly lifts up the tablecloth and looks for the diner's nonexistent rat. I shove Walter into my bag before he has a chance to run.

"Martina, sit up," Mom scolds from the next table. "Use your manners, *presidenta.*"

I smooth the tablecloth back down; she shoots me a wink that lets me know she's not really mad.

After coffee and dessert—grilled apples with cinnamon—everyone finally makes their way home.

My abuelita takes my hand and asks me what my first act as president of the student council will be. I tell her I ran on a platform of learning outside the classroom, so I'll be taking suggestions for our first field trip.

"Maybe the ballet," my abuelita suggests.

"I've always thought there's nothing better than watching someone dance." Her eyes twinkle as she hugs me goodbye.

Does my abuelita know about Walter? My family is more mysterious—and fun—than any sticker, hands down. (Especially if that sticker is a soccer player with red hair, freckles, and a habit of stealing best friends.)

our First meeting

Last week, Caitlyn was one of the first to congratulate me on a good campaign, but I'm a little nervous about seeing Tommy. Will he be mad I won the election? Will I be the new target of his constant joking? The thought of being the punch line of lame knock-knock jokes for the rest of the year makes me want to hide under the covers and pretend to be sick.

Craig, of course, won't stand for this kind of moping. "Come on! Time to start the day, Madame President!"

I jump up when I realize Walter is snuggled next to me on the pillow. The chipmunk is as skittish as I am and immediately leaps into first position. He grabs onto the spindle of my headboard and begins a series of warm-ups.

"Stretching is *key*," Walter says between leg lifts. "Starting the day without warming up is worse than not eating breakfast."

"Unless breakfast is a pastry," Craig adds.

Walter motions for Craig to join in, but Craig wants nothing to do with morning exercises.

"Martina, let's go!" Walter says.

I decide that stretching with a chipmunk probably makes more sense than hiding under the covers and worrying about Tommy, who I can't control. I wonder if someone like Bev deals with this kind of mental tug-of-war before her day starts too.

After breakfast, I hide Craig in my backpack and head to school. Walter is unhappy he doesn't get to come along, but I remind him of the ruckus he caused at the diner and how much trouble I'd get into if he did that in the classroom.

I take the piece of fabric and the plywood off the top of the treasure chest and dangle Walter over the shiny stones. He can't help but *oooohhhh* at the glistening jewels.

"It's a visual feast!" Walter pirouettes across the colorful gems.

"That should keep him busy," Craig says. "But you're stalling, Martina! Get to school!"

Is it weird that the person who knows me best isn't a person at all, but a cupcake?

When I get to school, several kids congratulate me, and it turns out Tommy couldn't be nicer. It's almost as if his mind moved past the election five minutes after it happened. I can't imagine having a mind that doesn't cling to and worry about every single thing that happens in a day. I may have won the election, but I'm the person who's envious today. How does Tommy do it?

Classes fly by quickly, which is usually great news for a Monday, but my anxiety about our first student council meeting makes me want to slow the day to a crawl. At the final bell, when most kids are on their way home or to activities, I head to the multipurpose room to meet up with the others.

At my old school, anyone from class could attend student council meetings, but here it's only the elected officials and Ms. Graham. I know Mike, and hopefully it will be fun getting to know Scott and Samantha too. Mike is his usual carefree self, but Scott is taking his treasurer role so seriously, he brought in an old-fashioned calculator from home. As we talk about how much our plans might cost, Scott pounds away on the number keys. I'm not sure if what he's typing is real or gibberish, but he sure seems to be working hard.

"We do need bigger cubbies," Mike says. "But I think a field trip is the most important thing. What do you guys think?"

Samantha, Scott, and I agree and share our ideas. We discuss everything from the La Brea

Tar Pits to the California Science Center to a Kings game to the Santa Monica Pier.

I save my best option for last. "There's a new panda exhibit coming to the Los Angeles Zoo next week," I say. "With two baby pandas!"

"I saw it on the news," Samantha says. "They're adorable!"

Scott tucks his pencil behind his ear as if that might help him think. "I'm pretty sure there's a monkey exhibit too."

I want to respect Scott's suggestion, but we're talking baby pandas here! Luckily, Samantha and Mike feel the same way I do, and it takes less than a minute to convince Scott that baby pandas are WAY more exciting than regular monkeys. Ms. Graham thinks our class will be thrilled with our first excursion.

By the time we finish the meeting, most everyone else has left for the day, so Samantha and I walk out together to wait for our rides. It may sound ridiculous, but for some reason I thought being on student council might suddenly make my shyness go away. I just spent over an hour as president of my class and feel totally the same— just with more work to do.

"Suppose when we tell the class, no one wants to go to the zoo?" I ask Samantha.

"What are you talking about? The zoo's a great idea! Stop doubting yourself."

It's difficult to explain worrying to someone who doesn't. I remember at my old school, when Chris Tobin and I were in charge of the refreshments for the class Halloween party. Even though I reminded him twice the day before not to forget the apple juice, I made my mom buy two extra gallons in case Chris forgot.

"What makes you think he'll forget?" Mom asked. "Maybe all you need to worry about are the cookies *you* have to bring."

But I was nervous about my part of the job AND Chris's. He laughed when he saw me carrying the heavy bag of juice into the classroom the next morning and pointed to the plastic bottles he'd already placed on the table. He didn't seem angry that I didn't trust him to do his part, but he shoved the juice I brought underneath the table next to the trash. When Mom asked about it, I didn't want her to think I wasted money, so I told her Chris DID forget the juice. I felt bad lying, but I didn't feel like having another "chat" about how it's not good to worry all the time. And here I am, a year later, at a different school, with different kids, doing the same thing.

"Everything's going to be fine." Samantha smiles like she wants me to be happy, not like I'm doing something wrong. So I smile back and tell her it's going to be the best field trip in the history of field trips.

After Samantha climbs into her mom's SUV, Craig pops out of my bag. "Don't bite off more than you can chew on this field trip."

"Funny advice coming from a cupcake. Samantha's right—everything will be great."

But as soon as I say it, it's not true. I suddenly spot Bev and Eileen on the soccer field across the street, running balls toward a goal. They're

laughing as they race through the orange cones, having a blast.

For once, Craig's voice isn't sarcastic, but kind. "It's hard when you're not included, isn't it?"

"My best friend would rather hang out with one of my stickers than with me."

"Your best friend IS a sticker," Craig says. "And he's right here."

When Dad pulls into the pickup lane, I get in the car and turn away from the field. But it's like watching an accident on the other side of the highway—it's impossible to look away.

I watch Bev and Eileen race across the grass until Dad's car turns the corner and their images vanish from view.

An
Afternoon
with James

When I get home, my parents have a meeting with their accountant, so I have to stay with James till they get back. I actually like it when James and I are the only ones home. Without Eric walking around the house with earbuds, having loud phone conversations with his friends, I can play with my two-year-old brother in peace.

It's embarrassingly fun to sit on the floor and amuse myself with the same games I enjoyed when I was a toddler. First, James and I make the Mary Poppins puzzle with the oversized pieces that my abuelita gave me for my third birthday and that James now loves. Then I try to teach James hide-and-seek and duck, duck, goose, but they're more difficult and less fun with only two people.

While I help him dip celery stalks into peanut butter, I think about how much fun it would be to share my magical stickers with James. Even though he probably only knows a few hundred words, I can't take the chance of him blabbing to my parents. But how cool would it be to fly around the valley at sunset in a hot-air balloon with my little brother?

When he's done with his snack, James chases Lily around the coffee table and couch as if it's his own personal racetrack. I *really* want to play with my stickers. Can I pretend any of them are a toy?

I grab the palette and brush, which I haven't used since my poster party. Even after wetting them at the sink, the paints are dried up and useless. (Like they were in my campaign.)

"I *love* your brother," Walter whispers when James zips by us. "He's got such great energy."

I smooth Walter's tail, which looks like it might've been dragged through the pool of shampoo Eric left on the bathroom floor. "You can hang out with us," I say. "But you absolutely cannot talk to James!"

Walter looks around, clearly not happy. After a minute, he finally says okay. "It will give me a chance to practice my interpretive dancing."

"Not a word!" I repeat.

Walter uses his tiny hand and pretends to zip his mouth shut.

"Look what I found!" I bring Walter out from behind my back and place him in front of James.

With the most care I've ever seen him use, James gently pets Walter on the top of the head. Walter's right foot bounces against the table with pleasure.

Walter's about to talk, but as soon as I give him the evil eye, he stops.

"This is a chipmunk," I say. "His name is Walter."

"Walter ride in wagon." James scoops up Walter from the table and places him in his little plastic wagon.

James thankfully doesn't race through the house the way he usually does, but carefully pulls Walter from room to room, talking to him the whole time. It's the kind of scene that would be great to video, but since I don't have a phone, I can't. I run into my room to get the

phone that used to be a sticker, but it doesn't take a picture this time either. USELESS! The phone makes me think of calling Bev. Or is she still playing soccer with Eileen?

I suddenly hear something crash down the hall and I freeze. Is someone trying to break into the house? I hurry toward James—should we run over to Ms. Henley's and call my parents? But when the next sound is a grunt, I cautiously tiptoe to my room.

Zombie Boy is going through my desk.

"What are you doing?" I grab Eric's fedora from Zombie Boy's head. I take the purple marker from his hand and return it to the coffee mug on my desk.

Zombie Boy grunts and takes the orange marker instead.

Not only has Zombie Boy gone through my desk, he's taken a stack of my sacred neon index cards. I hold out my hand and he gives them to me. They've all been neatly printed with the letters *DJDK*. I point to the text and ask him to

explain, but he just grunts.

Craig looks over my shoulder at the card. "DJDK—*DJ Decay*! Get it? It's actually kind of funny. He's great with music AND with marketing!"

I check on James and Walter, who are now reading picture books on the couch. When I get back to my room, I motion for Zombie Boy to take off his headphones.

"I don't know why you need business cards, but you have to get back to the garage before my little brother sees you."

What's that noise? The sound of car doors— my parents!

James is now the least of my problems. I rush

Zombie Boy out the back just as my parents unlock the front door.

"Chipmunk!" James says. "Chipmunk dance!"

Walter bounds toward my parents and my mother screams.

"How did a chipmunk get in the house?" Dad asks. "Is the garage door open?"

"NO!" I block the back door, then realize I have to take my panic down a notch. "The chipmunk was scratching at the back door, so I let him in. He's harmless, but I'll put him outside."

Mom picks up James and washes his hands at the sink. "You have to be more careful, Martina. Rodents carry diseases—you two could get sick!"

I tell Mom she's right and usher Walter outside.

"Diseases! What is she talking about?" Walter shrieks. "I can't stay out here too long."

I tell him I'll bring him back inside as soon as my parents fall asleep.

Walter points to Zombie Boy tucked into the corner of the garage, bopping his head to the music on his laptop as he creates more business cards.

"He only eats brains, right?" Walter asks. "Not ballerinas?"

I'm beginning to think my life was easier before I had magic stickers.

A TOO-COOl PARTY

Samantha, Scott, Mike, and I got approval for the field trip to the Los Angeles Zoo, but because tickets for the baby pandas are selling so fast, Ms. Graham moves up the trip before the exhibit sells out. The baby pandas are all anyone can talk about, even though the student council has accomplished other things as well. Scott and his dad found a dance studio that was going out of business and offered our class their cubbies for a dollar each—a total bargain. The stainless-steel baskets are in great shape, and Ms. Graham lets us spend the free period replacing our old cubbies with the new baskets. Stephanie's mom runs an upholstery business, so Stephanie brought in four big square pillows to use in the reading loft, and for the window seat I donated some striped fabric Mom had. Mike borrowed a floor lamp from his dad's home office and plugged it in between the bookshelves.

"Your new student council has transformed our reading loft!" Ms. Graham tells the class. "I'm so glad you elected such a take-charge group!"

Bev whips around in her seat and gives me a big smile. Eileen isn't with her today, which is good—although I hope Eileen isn't getting into trouble that I'll have to get her out of later.

I've been so busy with student council these last few days that I've had less time to do things with Bev. It's great to hang out by the picnic table at recess and research pandas during library time.

I haven't minded staying after school for the

meetings lately, but today I'd rather leave with Bev and go over to her house. The student council has a lot of details to get through before the trip, and I don't want to let the other members down.

Ms. Graham tells us again how happy she is with the job we're doing and helps us make sure everything's ready for the big day.

"Best field trip in the history of field trips," Samantha reminds me afterward.

I wasn't serious when I said it, but I'm beginning to think that actually might be the case. After the meeting, I wait outside for Eric to pick me up. Now that he has his license, he's supposed to help my parents out with the driving, but what it means for me is that I spend a lot of time *waiting.*

I stick my head back into the school to check the time. Reason #27 why I should have my own cell phone.

Cell phone!

I feel around in my bag for the cell phone that

used to be a sticker. Being stranded at school technically counts as an emergency, right? The magic cell phone *has* to work this time.

The screen lights up, but as I enter Eric's number and press the CALL button, nothing happens—again.

I throw the useless phone back in my bag and stand on my toes to see if Mrs. Spurlock is still in the office so I can use her phone. But I'm almost knocked over by the sound of tires screeching to a halt on the blacktop. Sure enough, Eric skids into the pickup lane in my mother's Chevy.

"You were supposed to be here at four!" I say. "Mom's going to kill you!"

"If she finds out, which she won't, cuz you're not going to tell her." Eric turns the volume louder on the radio so he can't hear me complain.

"I have to make a stop first," he says. "There's a big party at Jessica's and I told her I'd drop some stuff off."

"I don't want to go to a party—I want to go home!"

"You are most definitely *not* going to the party," Eric says. "Only cool kids are invited."

It wasn't that long ago that Eric used to sit next to me on the couch and explain basketball and football games, pick me up when I fell off my bike, and let me have the last bit of cereal at the bottom of the box. But this year, the only Eric I get is the grouchy one.

He turns left toward the high school, holding the steering wheel with the palm of his hand the way Dad does. After a few blocks, he pulls in front of a house with a line of cars parked out

front. "Wait here. Do NOT get out of the car."

"Don't worry, I have no interest in spying on your party." I fold my arms across my chest to emphasize the point.

Eric takes a tray covered with foil from the backseat; he obviously got Dad to contribute some snacks. Smelling the sausage and onions makes me realize I'm starving. I lift the foil off the tray as he slides it out of the car, but Eric is too fast and heads to the house before I can get a nibble.

I lean my head out the window. The field trip is in three days and I want everything to be perfect. It was great that Ms. Graham was so happy with our work in the classroom today, but the real test will be outside the class. I lean farther back and make a wish that the day will go smoothly.

From where I sit, I hear music that sounds familiar yet new. Where have I heard it before? I climb out of the car and head to the long, modern house at the top of the driveway. I look through the living room window at kids who go to school with Eric. Several of them are dancing to the familiar beat, including my brother as he balances the tray of food. I hold my hand above my eyes as a shield from the lights and am shocked when I see who's playing the music at this super-fun party.

Zombie Boy!

My brother will *kill* me, but I have to go inside and get my zombie sticker. How did he get here? Is he wearing Eric's fedora again? And most important—why is one of my stickers more popular than I am? Make that TWO of my stickers.

I quietly walk in and squeeze through the wall of dancing kids. Zombie Boy's in the corner, wearing his headphones, cuing up the next song on his laptop.

"What are you doing?" I ask. "We have to go home!"

Zombie Boy excitedly tilts his screen toward me and starts typing.

Then the computer starts *talking*.

"I wrote some code so you could understand me," Zombie Boy says. "How do you like my new voice?"

His voice doesn't sound robotic, but almost like a regular kid's.

"Jessica saw one of my flyers and asked me to be in charge of music," Zombie Boy says.

"You hung up flyers?!"

"All over town. I've got a gig tomorrow night too."

I suddenly notice he's wearing a belt fashioned out of the sapphires and rubies from my treasure chest. A sticker who's a nerd, a music lover, *and* a craft whiz? Are *all* zombies this talented?

When I see Eric hurrying toward us, I hold my ground.

"What are YOU doing here?" Eric shouts. "I told you to wait in the car!"

My brother is suddenly distracted by the new song Zombie Boy cues up. He starts bouncing up and down like he's on a pogo stick. "Dude! This music is killer! You're as good as Jessica said you were."

"Thanks—glad you like it!" Zombie Boy types.

Eric breaks into a huge grin. "Hey! I have that same hat!"

Zombie Boy fist-bumps Eric, who then says

he's taking me home. When I ask if we can stay a little longer, he won't hear of it.

"Martina's your sister?" Zombie Boy asks. "She's the only person I'll take requests from."

Eric is impressed, but no one's more surprised than me.

Zombie Boy hands me his laptop and tells me to pick the next song. I choose one of Eric's favorites, which buys me a little more time.

I hand the laptop back to Zombie Boy.

"Thanks for helping me come to life," he says. "I hate not being able to play my music."

I can't say for sure because his skin is green, but it looks like Zombie Boy is *blushing*.

OMG—does my zombie sticker

have A crush on me?

The BUS Ride

The next days are full of meetings, permission slips, and general panda excitement. Four parents volunteer to come as chaperones; Mom says she is happy to take the day off from work to accompany us but that James will have to tag along. The thought of my hyperactive brother coming doesn't make me happy, but having Mom around in case anything goes wrong does.

Even though my title on the student council is president, I could just as well be called Official Worrier. Every night, I run through scenarios of what could go wrong, driving Craig and Walter crazy in the process. Zombie Boy even made a playlist of songs for me to listen to and relax. The music he chose worked like a charm, and when the day of the field trip finally arrives I actually am excited and somewhat calm.

My abuelita sees us off in the school parking lot along with two friends of hers I haven't met before. (For someone who lives alone, my grandmother meets more new people in a day than everyone else I know combined.) One of the women looks familiar; it turns out her name is April and she owns the dry-cleaning shop I sometimes go to with Mom. April can't stop telling me about the baby pandas we'll be seeing later today. She and her grandchildren saw the exhibit at the National Zoo in Washington, D.C., and it was the highlight of their visit.

After much debate, Craig insisted on coming, but I'm shocked when I reach for his plastic container and find Walter inside my bag too.

"You can't dance up and down the aisles of the school bus," I tell the chipmunk. "Somebody could step on you."

"She just doesn't want to get in trouble," Craig tells Walter. "It's typical Martina."

I shoot him a look to keep quiet and take some celery out of my snack bag for Walter.

"I LOVE adventure," Walter says. "And I hear Eileen is coming too!"

Wait, what?

Before I can ask for details, Bev climbs onto the bus with Eileen.

"You didn't tell me your new friend was coming," Mom says.

I don't tell Mom that Eileen isn't really my friend and I didn't know she was coming either. Bev waves to me as if nothing is wrong, says hi to my mom as she passes us, then plops alongside Eileen in an empty seat in back.

Mom must sense something because she pulls me in for a quick hug.

"Today's going to be great," she says. "You did a wonderful job planning this trip."

For the first time since I've had my magic stickers, I want them all to go back to the sheet and never come alive again, even if that includes Walter and Craig. Why did I think having another sheet of magical stickers would be as fantastic as the first time?

"Okay," Ms. Graham says. "Off to the zoo!" She signals the bus driver, who closes the bifold doors. Parents wave from the parking lot as kids yell goodbye.

After we get through the worst parts of the morning traffic, Mom motions toward the back of the bus. "Why don't you go hang out with Bev?" she says. "Everything's under control here."

Mom nudges me in the gentle way she's been doing my whole life. I don't want to disappoint her, so I slowly make my way down the aisle.

I take the empty seat across from Bev. Eileen is lightly snoring against the window, probably exhausted from all that soccer. Or maybe they were up late last night, watching YouTube videos like Bev and I used to do.

The last thing I want is to start off on the wrong foot with Bev, but my words blurt out before I can stop them. "Eileen doesn't have a permission slip," I say. "She didn't sign up."

Bev looks at me strangely before she answers. I don't blame her; I sound like a tattletale.

"Lisa's aunt is in the hospital, so she's not here," Bev explains. "Since there was an extra space, Eileen asked if she could come. My mom called the school this morning and added her to the list."

Lots of thoughts bounce around my head: couldn't Bev have called me first to tell me? How is the president of our class the last one to know about new kids signing up for our trip? I don't want to be a wet blanket on Bev's new friendship, but where do *I* fit in?

"I'm not sure you should be getting so involved with Eileen," I say. "You know what happens to the stickers sooner or later—they all end up going back."

Bev shrugs in her easygoing way. "At least we'll have fun while she's here. My offensive game has really improved—you should play with us!"

I want to say that I WOULD play if they'd ever ask me, but I bite my tongue instead.

A couple of rows in front of us, Tommy's rolled up his permission slip like a telescope and is talking like a pirate. "Avast, mateys! A few more miles."

"Tommy! Sit down," Ms. Graham says.

Tommy obliges. "Sorry, but I just can't wait to get a look at those pandas." He starts to chant *"Pan-da, Pan-da!"*

The rest of the class joins in, even my brother James, who struggles to get out of Mom's lap and grab a fat June bug flying through the bus.

Mike tries to grab it too, but the June bug dive-bombs Samantha, then Tommy. I watch as the bug eventually lands on Eileen's shoulder.

Bev and I share a smile at Eileen. Still asleep, she doesn't realize she's now a landing strip.

Eileen reaches up and carelessly swats her shoulder. Then she opens her eyes, jumps out of her seat, and screams.

"Get that thing away from me!"

It's a silly, babyish thing to do—it's only a June bug, after all—but Eileen is suddenly the center of attention. And all the interest from my class-mates makes her scream and flail even louder. I try not to let her see me roll my eyes as Tommy and Mike shoo the bug away.

I've played with stickers my whole life and consider myself an expert on them, but before my stickers came alive I had no idea they could be so DRAMATIC. After Eileen finally calms down, I return to my seat alongside Mom. *Sheesh.*

When we arrive at the zoo, I hurry off the bus to get everyone's lunches, as well as James's stroller. The bus driver starts to lift up the door to the cargo unit, but the first things I see inside are Zombie Boy's shoes.

I jump in front of the bus driver and thank him, then guide him away from the cargo hold. As soon as he leaves, I open the door the rest of the way and grab Zombie Boy. "What are you doing here?"

He looks at me and lets out a giant belch. That's when I notice all the empty paper lunch bags.

"You ate all our food! None of us brought money for lunch!"

Zombie Boy holds out a soggy crust of bread that looks like it used to be part of a tuna-fish sandwich. He smiles shyly and grunts. He did some accessorizing in our garage—he's now wearing Mom's old rollerblades and gardening gloves.

Before the zombie can answer me, Scott runs toward us, then stops when he sees Zombie Boy.

"Why did you hire a DJ for the field trip?" Scott asks. "That wasn't in the budget."

I tell Scott that Zombie Boy came on his own, free of charge.

"We've got bigger problems than that," Scott says. "The panda exhibit is closed!"

oh no!!!

Ms. Graham warned us that even with the pre-
paid tickets, the lines at the gate might be long.
But as I follow Scott from the parking lot to the
main gate, all I see are angry visitors.

"What do you mean, we can't see the pandas?" one woman shouts.

"This is a rip-off!" a man next to her yells.
"False advertising!"

A woman in khaki shorts, shirt, and a pith
helmet addresses the crowd with a megaphone.

Before she says a word, Mike sneaks beside me.

"Maybe we should've gone with one of the other field-trip options," he says. "This looks like trouble."

The zookeeper explains that a pipe burst inside the panda enclosure yesterday and the exhibit is closed while a crew works on repairs.

"Just because some water leaked, we can't see the pandas?" Tommy asks. "Totally unfair!"

"I'm sorry," the zookeeper says. "But there are still so many fine exhibits here." She suddenly puts her walkie-talkie to her ear and listens. "I've got to run. Believe it or not, there's a boy in a zombie costume rollerblading through the reptile room."

Disappointment spreads through the class. Even the parent chaperones seem upset.

This is not good.

"You have to say something, Martina," Samantha says.

"ME? Why can't YOU say something?" I ask.

Samantha looks at me like I've just sprouted wings. *"You're* the president—it's your job."

Running for class president might be the worst idea I've ever had in my life. Oh, that's right—it WASN'T my idea.

When I turn to look at Mom, I can tell she agrees with Samantha. But it's Tommy who makes me realize I really have to say something. He's adding fuel to the fire, riling everyone up.

"You guys should've voted for me," he says. "I'd NEVER let you down like this. We could be throwing spaghetti at each other instead of being turned away from baby pandas."

My courage comes from an unlikely source: Bev. She looks at me with an expression that tells me I can take on Tommy today. I could be imagining it, but Eileen seems to be encouraging me too.

"We're not being thrown out of the zoo," I tell my classmates. "The pandas are just ONE exhibit. There are over a thousand animals here!"

"As treasurer I can verify that's a big number," Scott adds.

"Who wants to see the monkeys?" I shout.

Mike's got my back as well. He starts chanting, "I DO!" Samantha, Bev, and Eileen join in too.

Ms. Graham finishes the head count, then suggests we have a snack and a bathroom break first.

We go through the turnstiles at the gate and make a beeline for the rest area. But a new wave of dread washes over me. Zombie Boy ate our lunches!

"We need to keep everyone focused on the positive," Bev says.

Bev just said "we"—does that mean we're still friends? Technically, Eileen is a much more authentic Sticker Girl than I am. Is that why Bev likes her more? Wait a minute—what am I talking about? I'M Sticker Girl. I know how to solve this lunch problem!

I leave the group, duck behind the gift shop, and pull out my magic sticker sheet. *Please let the pizza multiply!*

whoosh! **POOF! Bam!**

"Did somebody order a

PIZZA PARTY?"

I shout!

Samantha crosses her arms in front of her and asks what happened to our lunches. I tell her there was a leak in the cargo compartment and they were ruined. Luckily the pizza smells

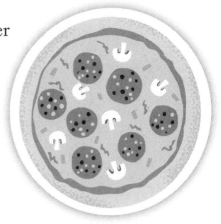

so good, no one thinks twice about their bag lunches.

Even though the sticker shows only one large pizza, when Bev, Mike, Samantha, and I hand out slices there's enough for everyone. The fact that the pizza doesn't run out is the first piece of good news today.

Ms. Graham takes a napkin from a dispenser on one of the picnic tables and uses it to blot the cheese on her slice. "I didn't realize lunch was

coming out of the budget today," Ms. Graham says.

"Neither did I," adds Scott. "We're definitely going to have to talk about this later."

Tommy eyes the line of people at the concession stand. "How did you get that pizza so fast, Martina?"

"Because while everyone else was complaining, Martina was getting things done," Bev says. "That's why we voted for her."

Bev's eyes twinkle as she hands me a slice. "Once a campaign manager, always a campaign manager," she whispers.

Just as I'm about to say thank you, Bev takes a seat next to Eileen.

Eileen beams. "I can't believe I'm going to have pizza for the first time! I've been waiting for this forever!"

The kids sitting at her table make a fuss about how Eileen has never had pizza before. I just saved the day, and here's Eileen making herself the center of attention. Again.

Everyone crowds around to watch Eileen take her first bite of pizza. She picks up the slice and sinks her teeth in. A gigantic smile spreads across her face.

"This is incredible!" Eileen says. "If Bev wasn't already my best friend, I'd want pizza to be!"

Did I hear that right?

Does Bev feel the same way?

I'm crushed. Running for student council isn't the worst idea I've ever had.

Being Sticker Girl is.

BUZZZZZZ!

The zookeeper who shows our class around is super nice; I'm not sure if it's to make up for the closed baby panda exhibit or if she's like this every day. On the way to the monkeys, she points out the zoo's newest members—a golden poison dart frog and a giant anteater. Tommy makes a joke about the giant anteater not looking gigantic at all, and Eileen laughs as if it's the funniest thing anyone's ever said.

I suddenly realize how annoying Eileen's laugh is—and how annoying everything else about her is too. I'm ashamed to admit it, but I actually dislike one of my own stickers.

As we enter the monkey exhibit, I get an idea to make Eileen the center of attention again— but not in a good way this time. If Eileen hates big, loud bugs buzzing around her, the smiling honeybee with the trumpet might be just the thing to make everyone else realize how desperate for attention Eileen really is.

I've never been a kid who pulled pranks before, but didn't Eileen just call Bev her BFF? And during the campaign, didn't Bev say we should always use the tools we have at our disposal? In that case . . . I fall behind the rest of the group and take the sheet of stickers from my bag.

This is going to be fun.

whoosh! Poof! Bam!

The honeybee

swirls above my head, obviously happy to be released. He hovers and swoops above the group, but when he gets near Eileen she doesn't even notice.

Maybe this plan isn't going to work after all.

But then the honeybee blows his horn.

"What was that?" the zookeeper asks. "Sounds like Darlene the Elephant might be ready for lunch!"

But it's not Darlene the Elephant. Suddenly a low hum begins in the distance. The humming gets louder and louder until a few kids cover their ears from the noise.

Scott sees them first. "BEES!" He points to a swarm of honeybees heading straight for us.

NOOOOOO! How was I supposed to know the honeybee sticker would use his trumpet to call thousands of his closest friends?

Eileen's not the only one who starts screaming; pretty much everyone else does too. The zookeeper waves her arms to try to disperse the swarm, then reaches for her walkie-talkie to call for help.

There are so many bees swarming around us, you can barely see the sky.

WHAT HAVE I DONE?

Mom protects James's head underneath her jacket, but he's still crying. So are several kids in my class (Tommy included). I duck down and rummage through my bag to find Craig.

"How do I stop this?" I scream.

"I have no idea!" he answers. "But keep those bees away from my frosting!"

It was wrong to try to scare Eileen—I know that. But how do I fix this?

Our conversation is interrupted by Caitlyn,

who's screaming even louder than the rest of us. "I'm allergic to bees!"

Ms. Graham pulls Caitlyn aside and helps her find the EpiPen in her bag. Thankfully Caitlyn is more prepared for this emergency than I am.

But none of us are prepared for the monkeys,

who are now in a frenzy over the swarming insects.

"Look out!" The zookeeper points to three monkeys jumping up and down on the roof of the exhibit. One of them leaps off the building and lands in the middle of our group. It might actually be cool—if we weren't being attacked by a zillion bees.

The zookeeper tries to calm the monkey with her soothing voice, but he's too wound up from all the buzzing. Other monkeys jump down to join him.

The first monkey pulls off Tommy's Lakers

cap and tries it on, which actually makes Mike laugh.

Then another monkey grabs the EpiPen away from Caitlyn and races up the nearest tree.

And there's nothing funny about that at all.

walter to the Rescue

As the swarm of bees moves toward the reptile house, Ms. Graham hurries Caitlyn into the zoo-keeper's office to keep her safe. The chaperones run through several options. Rush us all back to the bus? Retrieve Caitlyn's medicine? Call it a day?

Tommy's the first one with a suggestion. "You should use a tranquilizer dart on those monkeys!" he tells the zookeeper. "I can shoot it if you want!"

Two other zookeepers enter the exhibit and

use calm voices to coax the monkey down from the palm tree, but he climbs even higher.

I feel a tugging on my skirt and look down to see Walter.

"Let me go up and get her medicine," he whispers. "I'll be back in a jiff."

Craig agrees. "Walter's the only one here who can climb that high."

"Who said anything about climbing? I'm going to *dance* my way up that tree!"

I shield Walter and Craig so none of my classmates will see them. "The last thing we need right now is a chipmunk in a tutu!"

"Or is it the FIRST thing?" Before I can stop him, Walter leaps to the tree but is immediately stopped by the monkeys guarding the trunk. Luckily my classmates are all focused on the top of the tree and no one notices Walter sneaking up the back.

Using his best moves, Walter weaves and dodges, but unfortunately his fancy footwork is no match for the primates.

"What are we going to do?" Bev asks.

She looks as worried as I am; I'm just glad she doesn't know *I'm* the one to blame for this nightmare.

Walter's sweating and out of breath when he jumps back into my bag. "Those monkeys are *monsters*," he says. "I don't know how we're going to get that medicine."

Bev and I watch the zookeepers place a ladder against the tree. It looks like they might finally make some progress—until the monkeys knock it down.

Think, think, think!

I run to Eileen and ask if she brought her soccer ball.

"Of course—I bring it everywhere. You should know that if you call yourself Sticker Girl." From the look on her face, I can tell Eileen knows I'M the one who released the honeybees. "I could've told you that bee was trouble."

I want to make Eileen promise she won't share that particular piece of information with Bev, but right now there are more important things to worry about.

"Your aim with that ball is incredible," I tell her. "Do you think you can knock the pen out of the monkey's hand?"

Eileen gauges how far it is to the top of the tree, then holds out the ball and kicks. The ball sails over us, heading straight for the monkey—who then jumps even farther up the palm tree.

"It was a great try, Eileen." Bev then turns to me. "A good idea too."

But I don't deserve Bev's compliment—I got us into this mess and it's my job to get us out.

Craig and Walter peek out from my bag. "There *is* something else you could try." Craig nudges the sheet of magic stickers toward my hand.

My eyes lock with Bev's. The hot-air balloon!

"You can sail to the top of the tree and save the day," Bev says.

"*We* can." I look at the large group of people around us. How am I going to explain a giant hot-air balloon appearing out of thin air? I guess I'll have to worry about that later.

I peel off the last sticker on my sheet. Please be the answer to our problems!

whoosh! Poof! Bam!

The hot-air balloon

magically comes to life!

Sadly, the basket's the size of a cereal bowl.
How will my idea
even work now?

Quite the show

"So much for that," Bev says. "And here come the bees!"

I've been so focused on getting Caitlyn's medicine, I barely noticed that the bees moved to another part of the zoo. But given how today is going, OF COURSE they're back.

Samantha almost knocks me over. "You said this was going to be the best field trip in the history of field trips, but it's the WORST! What are we going to do?" She looks at the small hot-air balloon in my hand. "This is no time for toys, Martina!"

"It's not her fault there was a bee attack!" Bev says.

"It's not?" Eileen smirks. "Are you sure?"

I watch Bev's expression change.

"There *was* a bee on your sticker sheet," she says. "Did *you* release that swarm, Martina?"

"What do you mean?" Samantha asks.

Before I can answer either of them, Ms. Graham makes an announcement to the class, telling us to walk—not run—to the gift shop to take cover. She says Caitlyn's fine and as soon as the swarm disperses, we'll head back to the bus. As we line up, Bev looks at me like she's still waiting for an answer. How do I tell her this is all my fault?

I can feel Walter bouncing around in my bag, trying to get my attention. When I sneak a peek, he points to the miniature hot-air balloon in my hand. "Do you think it'll hold me?"

I tell him it's too dangerous, that I don't want

him to get hurt. "Besides, Caitlyn's in the gift shop."

Walter shakes his head. "She's okay now—but what if a bee flies inside? We need to get that EpiPen back." Walter motions to the balloon with his tiny hand.

"You just want to ride in a hot-air balloon," I say. "This has nothing to do with Caitlyn's medicine."

"Who DOESN'T want to ride in a hot-air balloon?" Walter asks. "Who DOESN'T want to save the day?"

While Mom ushers the rest of the class inside, I try to spot the original bee with the trumpet. Where is that troublemaker? But I can't tell him apart from the hundreds of others in the sky. I swat several bees away as we talk.

"I think you should let Walter go," Craig says. "In case Caitlyn needs the medicine later."

I look at the tiny hot-air balloon—Walter might be able to fit inside. As soon as he sees me

waver, Walter takes the opportunity to jump inside the basket. What will happen if I let go?

"There's only one way to find out," Craig says, reading my mind yet again.

I tell Walter to be careful, then let go of the balloon. It slowly lifts into the air.

"The monkeys will stop you," Craig tells him.

Walter motions to the telephone lines near the palm tree. "If this balloon can get me to those lines, I'll do the rest."

The balloon jerkily rises above my head, and I'm surprised to see Bev standing beside me.

"It might work," she says. "Walter is someone I'd put money on."

I want to tell her I'm sorry I've been acting so weird, and sorry I unleashed bees on our class. But most of all I want to tell her I miss hanging out with her and hope that we're still friends.

But before I can say anything, Samantha runs outside with several other kids trailing behind her.

"Look at that chipmunk in your balloon!" Samantha yells. "Is he . . . wearing a tutu? This zoo is insane!"

The zookeeper comes outside, shielding her eyes from the sun. A crowd gathers around the tree full of monkeys too.

The three monkeys on the trunk of the palm tree try to grab Walter as he sails by, but they can't reach him. When the tiny balloon reaches the telephone lines, Walter hops out. The balloon continues to float to the ground while Walter carefully balances himself on the wire.

Several people take videos of this strange chipmunk in a tutu making his way across a telephone wire as if it's a tightrope. Except Walter isn't walking.

He's *dancing*.

Walter glides, leaps, spins, and pirouettes across the telephone line as if onstage. He may be a chipmunk, but he's one hundred percent ham. It's uncanny! Everyone on the ground is silent, staring at the incredible performance overhead. Even the monkey with Caitlyn's medicine seems transfixed. He watches from the top of the tree as Walter bounces on the wire, leaps into the sky, and soars through the air. As his finale, the chipmunk whisks the EpiPen out of the monkey's unsuspecting hand while the crowd below goes wild.

Furious, the monkey lunges at Walter, who dives behind a group of palm fronds. The other primates shriek and race to the top of the tree, but now Walter's the one in charge. Everyone cheers as Walter zips by the angry monkeys and down the trunk of the tree. With a low bow, he neatly deposits the medicine into my hands.

"That was crazy!" Mike says. "I've got to come here more often!"

Samantha's not so sure. "How did a random chipmunk happen to know we were trying to get back Caitlyn's medicine?" She looks around the benches and exhibits. "And where's the chipmunk now?"

I can feel Walter trembling with exhaustion

inside my bag. "I'm sure he's around here some-where," I answer.

"How do you know it's a 'he'?" Samantha shakes her head. "And how does a chipmunk get a tutu?"

"Didn't you see the sign for the rodent ballet when we came in?" Bev asks. "The gerbil who does *Swan Lake* is an internet sensation."

I don't know how Bev does it, but she gets Samantha to stop asking questions—at least for now.

Ms. Graham makes sure Caitlyn stays inside while the zookeepers gather up the monkeys.

Zombie Boy skates to a halt beside me. "You want me to get rid of these bees for good?"

"Do zombies eat bees?" I ask.

"Don't be ridiculous!" He sets up his laptop in the middle of the swarm.

"This is no time for music!" I shout above the humming of the bees.

Zombie Boy begins to play a melodic beat of

low beeps and hums. It reminds me of the music they play at the salon where Mom gets her hair done.

"Music is calming to lots of animals," the zookeeper says. "Your DJ friend might be on to something."

Geeky Zombie Boy has a pretty great brain for someone who could probably function without one. The bees slow down, and after a few minutes the swarm disperses as the bees drift farther and farther away. In a few minutes more, they're completely gone.

Ms. Graham cautiously leads Caitlyn outside, then lines all of us up to make sure we're okay. Everyone is excited, Caitlyn most of all. I guess she's not that different from Eileen—she almost *liked* the attention.

"Well, THAT was a first," the zookeeper says. "Swarming bees, belligerent monkeys, and a ballet-dancing chipmunk. What's next?"

"How about if we let ALL the animals out

and then try to get them back in?" Tommy suggests.

"I've got a better idea." The zookeeper's face breaks into a smile. "How about a private showing of the baby panda exhibit?"

WHAT?! A wave of excitement rolls through our class.

"The plumbers have finished fixing the leak, so the exhibit can officially open this weekend. But what if I *unofficially* take you over there now?"

With everyone so wound up, it takes a moment for me to realize Eileen and Bev have grabbed my hands and are pulling me toward the exhibit. We hurry down the private access road with the rest of the class, toward the pandas.

I slow down for a second to check on Walter. He's lying in my bag while Craig fans him with a tissue. He looks exhausted.

I tell Walter he saved the day.

"But how was the dance?" he asks. "Original? Thrilling?"

When I tell him it was the most original and thrilling dance any of us have ever seen, Walter smiles—then immediately dozes off.

I catch up to Bev and Eileen. We're just a few steps away from the baby pandas!

A Day to Remember

Because they're only six months old, the pandas are still a bit wobbly on their feet and have just started to eat solid food—which of course means bamboo. Before that, they subsisted on only their mother's milk and sleep. James is fascinated by the pandas and strains against Mom's arms to join them in the enclosure.

"This one is Lin Pi and the other is Mei Pan."
The zookeeper holds up the smaller of the two.
"Aren't they the cuddliest?"

We beg the zookeeper to let us hold the pandas, but she tells us it's against regulations. "How about if *I* hold her and we get someone in here to take a class picture?" she says.

As we gather around the baby pandas for a class photo, Mike looks about to jump out of his skin. "This is *amazing*," he says.

Even Tommy agrees. "A monkey stole my hat, we got attacked by killer bees, a chipmunk danced across a power line, and we're the only ones at the zoo who get to see the baby pandas. This day is epic!"

"Best field trip in the history of field trips," Stephanie adds.

The three zookeepers arrange us around the pandas, then take several pictures. Ms. Graham can't stop thanking the staff for all they've done. We eventually say goodbye and head back to the school bus.

Because I'm president, Ms. Graham asks me to help out by doing a second head count. I stand outside the bus, counting as everyone takes a seat.

Craig pops out of my bag. "You're avoiding Bev," he says. "Don't you think you need to talk to her?"

I tell him that everything's fine. But Craig's not letting me off the hook. "Friendship takes work," he says. "Even a cupcake knows that."

Walter sticks his head out, groggy from sleep. "I'm with Craig on this."

"You guys are making me lose count!" I watch Eileen and Bev take a seat in the back just as Zombie Boy skates up to the cargo hold.

"You sure you'll be okay in there?" I ask.

He grabs a handful of soiled lunch bags and pops them into his mouth. "I love it here," he says between bites. "Totally comfortable."

When everyone is accounted for, I climb aboard, taking a seat next to my mom.

As we pull out of the parking lot, no one can keep quiet.

"That was awesome!"

"Incredible!"

"Best day of my life!"

I'm thrilled my classmates enjoyed the field trip, but I can't help feeling Craig and Walter are right. I DO have unfinished business. I make my way down the aisle of the bus and squeeze into the seat with Bev and Eileen.

It takes a moment for me to find the words, but I eventually do. "I'm really sorry I was acting so weird and jealous. I just felt left out and didn't know what to do."

Bev looks at me and smiles. "You're a great friend, Martina. But that doesn't mean I don't like hanging out with other kids too."

"I know—I just didn't want to stop being friends, that's all."

"Why would we stop being friends?" Bev asks. "That's never going to happen."

I tell her it was wrong to prank Eileen and treat her like an enemy. Every magic sticker I've had has taught me something, maybe Eileen most of all.

I feel a rumbling in my bag; I open it slowly so I won't wake Walter in case he's sleeping again.

"Martina—it's time to go," Craig says.

"Go where?" I ask. "We're almost back at school."

"No, I mean GO." Craig holds up the sheet of stickers. The treasure chest, pizza, bee, and paint palette are already back on the sheet.

When I jump up, the bus driver immediately tells me to sit down.

"NO! You can't leave! You just got here! There are so many things we need to do!" I beg.

Craig shakes his frosted head. "Sorry, but we don't have any choice. You know that."

"No, no, no!"

I watch Walter go from sleeping next to my wallet back to the sheet of stickers.

I whip around to face Eileen. "We got off on the wrong foot. I'm so sorry! Please stay!"

Eileen grabs my hand, then Bev's. "It was a blast hanging out—with BOTH of you."

Before I can ask how we're going to explain her disappearance to Ms. Graham, Eileen is back on the sheet with the other stickers. Zombie Boy too.

I examine the sticker sheet. Every sticker except the cupcake is back in position. Bev puts her hand on my arm.

"Goodbye, Craig," I whisper. "Maybe I'll see you around?"

"Not if I see you first." Craig winks and jumps back onto the sheet of stickers.

"Maybe one of them will get left behind like last time," Bev says.

But when I look at the sheet, they're all there.

Can you still be Sticker Girl if you no longer have magic stickers?

one more Thing

When we get back to the school parking lot, Ms. Graham takes another head count to make sure everyone's here.

"Where's your friend Eileen?" she asks Bev.

"Actually, she's *our* friend," I tell Ms. Graham. "She decided not to go to our school after all. Her mom just picked her up." I point to a car pulling into the street.

"What about that DJ in the zombie getup?" Mom adds. "I was going to see if he wanted to play at your father's birthday party next week."

I tell her that, sadly, DJDK took off too.

Tommy sticks his head into the group and holds out one of Zombie Boy's handmade business cards. "I've got his number, Mrs. Rivera. I was going to call him too."

"Good luck with that," Bev whispers.

For the next week, all anyone can talk about is how much fun our class had at the zoo. I know I should be basking in praise the way my student council classmates are, but I'm too busy worrying about our next event. After this trip, anything else will be a giant disappointment.

"You worry too much!" Bev tells me as we watch YouTube clips at my house that weekend. "The next trip will be even more fun. You just wait!"

But my room feels empty without Craig, Walter, Zombie Boy, and even the fake-treasure-chest table. If I'm honest, I also miss Eileen always trying to grab the spotlight. Why did I let her get under my skin so much? I'm usually happy when other people want the spotlight, since I never do. I guess I have to learn to trust my friends more—even if they're stickers.

A phone rings in the distance; Bev and I ignore it and continue watching the video of the rat with the slice of pizza.

The phone continues to ring. Why isn't anyone picking it up?

I go to the kitchen and ask Dad if he's going to answer it. He looks at me over his reading glasses. "Answer what? I don't hear anything."

He motions toward his cell phone, which is sitting quiet on the counter.

I tell him it must be the landline. "Can't you hear it?"

My father turns to the phone in the kitchen, which also isn't ringing. "I don't hear anything, Marti."

Then where's that sound coming from?

When I get back to my room, Bev's looking under my books and clothes. "Wasn't one of the stickers on that last sheet a cell phone?"

"Yes, but it never worked."

Our eyes meet, and then we frantically tear apart my room.

"It was definitely on the sheet when they all disappeared," I say. "I saw it!"

"Where's the sheet?" Bev asks. "Where's the sheet?"

I ask Bev to give me a boost so I can reach the top shelf of my closet. I feel across the too-big clothes Mom got on sale that she's waiting for me to grow into. Aha! I jump back down and hand the sheet to Bev.

The cell phone sticker is no longer in its spot.

"It's here somewhere!" I say. "We have to find that phone!"

We run from room to room but can't pin down where the sound is coming from. First it seems to be coming from the living room, then the kitchen. We look under tables, chairs, and shelves but can't find it.

"Where could it be?" Bev asks.

I hold my finger to my lips and we both listen. Now the sound is even farther away.

"Where's it coming from?" Bev asks.

"The garage!" I grab Bev and we hurry out of the house.

We look through the area where Zombie Boy hung out, but the phone's not there. We both stop again to listen, then realize where the ringing is coming from.

Dad's suitcase!

We lay the suitcase on the ground and slowly unzip it. Sure enough, the phone that used to be a sticker is inside.

The second I pick it up, it stops ringing.

"Hello?" I say. "Is anybody there?"

Like before, the phone is dead.

I toss the cell back into the suitcase, disappointed. "Well, so much for that."

But when I look at Bev, she's grinning from ear to ear. I follow her eyes to the pocket on the inside of the suitcase.

Is it? No! It can't be!

Another sheet of stickers!

BONUS MATERIALS

GOFISH

JANET TASHJIAN

What did you want to be when you grew up?
When I was really young, I used to make a lot of clothes for my dolls out of felt. Back then, I thought about being a fashion designer.

What's your most embarrassing childhood memory?
Having my shoe come off onstage during a school recital.

What's your favorite childhood memory?
Being outside in summer, at the end of the day when the light changes. It's still my favorite time of day.

What was your favorite thing about school?
When the bell rang at three o'clock.

What was your least favorite thing about school?
The school uniforms didn't have pockets.

What were your hobbies as a kid? What are your hobbies now?
I used to sew a lot. I sew less now, but I still like to work with my hands.

What was your first job, and what was your "worst" job?
I did a lot of babysitting, of course, and waitressing. I also worked on an assembly line when I was sixteen—it wasn't as much fun as it looked on *I Love Lucy.*

How did you celebrate publishing your first book?
I did a book signing near my hometown, and my tenth-grade English teacher came. I hadn't seen her since high school; it was a real treat.

Where do you write your books?
At my house in LA, often sitting outside. The benefit of writing in longhand is that I can write anywhere, so I also go to coffee shops and restaurants to get out of the house.

Did you collect stickers as a kid? Do you collect them now?
I wasn't really a sticker kid but I did love Colorforms. I realize I'm dating myself with the reference, but I used to love creating scenes with the colorful plastic stickers (I still have a felt board too!). I did always cut things out of paper, felt and fabric, and I still love making collages; I just got some vintage paper dolls at a yard sale that I'll

do something with. So even though I don't buy a lot of stickers, I kind of make my own.

OMG—this is a tough one! I have piles of vintage fabric that I love but wouldn't be that much fun alive. I also have a TON of board games but I'm not sure how much fun they'd be either. I *do* have a lot of doll heads—they actually might be cool to bring to life. They'd probably complain about being stuck in a giant glass jar in my living room but they might also have some interesting things to say. Wait, what am I talking about—I have a unicorn raft in my pool! That's the one!

I was pretty quiet as a kid; I was definitely a bookworm. I blossomed into a chatterbox as I got older. I am definitely not shy now.

People say that leaders are readers, and I certainly think that's true. I've been reading several books a week since I was a kid; I can't imagine how much critical information I'd be missing if I DIDN'T read. I also think listening is very important, not just for leaders but for everyone. Listening may seem like a passive task, but ACTIVE listening—where you're really trying to hear someone else's point of view—is a real skill.

Martina may be shy, but introverted kids are often expert listeners. Finding out what her classmates are interested in is an important part of Martina getting elected.

Martina feels jealous when Bev and Eileen become close friends. Have you ever felt jealous of a friend? How did you overcome that feeling?
I think envy and jealousy often come up in friendships. Sometimes one of my friends will win a big award and I *might* get a twinge of jealousy, but it's important to remember that their success is a GOOD thing, not something to be worried about. Martina faces maybe the most difficult kind of envy, where you think your position as a BFF is in danger when someone new and exciting comes along. I wanted to look at how that kind of jealousy puts unnecessary strain and pressure on a friendship. Martina needs to trust that her friendship with Bev is strong enough to let others into their world. Envy is not just a girl thing either; in *My Life as a Stuntboy*, Derek gets to be in the movies, so he and Matt have to deal with these kind of issues too.

Did you ever run for student government? What advice would you give to kids thinking about running for student office?
I was secretary of my senior class in high school. Though looking back, I'm not sure what we did other than plan the prom! Several of my friends' kids are in student government now and my nieces have been too. Running for office is often seen as a popularity contest, but for those students who really want to fight for

change, there's lots that can be accomplished. In Martina's case, her big test is the class field trip; keeping calm and helping others is what she needs to do as a leader, and she does a good job.

After *The Gospel According to Larry* and *Vote for Larry* came out, I got letters from students around the world who were becoming activists and getting involved in their schools and communities, which made me very happy. I was just at an amazing Shepard Fairey exhibition in LA. The theme was that we as citizens can't afford to be apathetic. I couldn't agree more.

Of the books you've written, which is your favorite?

I love *Tru Confessions* because it was my first. I love *The Gospel According to Larry* because I really accomplished what I set out to do. I love *My Life as a Book* because I got to work with my son. There's something special about all my books.

What challenges do you face in the writing process, and how do you overcome them?

Writing books is a marathon and my personality is more like a sprinter's. I have to work very hard to stay on task. So I write every day with a clear goal of how much I need to get done.

Which of your characters is most like you?

There's a lot of me in Larry, for sure. I also relate to the mother in *My Life as a Book*. Trudy's ambition in *Tru Confessions* is also very me.

es you laugh out loud?
hilarious—makes me laugh out loud every

What do you do on a rainy day?
In LA, you don't get a lot of rainy days, so when it does rain, it's a great excuse to sit on the couch and watch movies.

What's your idea of fun?
Hanging out with friends, going to movies, discovering new places in the city, walking my dog on the bluff.

What's your favorite song?
I could never come up with just one favorite song. I love music and listen to it all day long. One song I could never live without is Frank Zappa's "Peaches en Regalia." It makes me smile every time I hear it.

Who is your favorite fictional character?
It would be impossible to choose.

What was your favorite book when you were a kid? Do you have a favorite book now?
I used to read a lot of Nancy Drew and Encyclopedia Brown books. When I got older, it was Kurt Vonnegut. I read a lot of nonfiction now, too.

What's your favorite TV show or movie?
I like *Modern Family* and *Glee*. My favorite movie of all time is *Chinatown*.

 SQUARE FISH

If you were stranded on a desert island, who would you want for company?
My husband, my son, and my dog—I couldn't imagine being there without them. I could stay on a desert island forever if they were there with me.

If you could travel anywhere in the world, where would you go and what would you do?
I've done a lot of traveling but have never been to South America, so I guess that would be next.

What's the best advice you ever received about writing?
Hemingway's advice that the most important thing about a first draft is to finish it. I live by that rule.

Do you ever get writer's block? What do you do to get back on track?
I hardly ever get writer's block; I have the opposite problem—so many stories rattle around in my mind that I have to constantly stay on task to finish one project without getting distracted by another one. But when I do get stuck, I use another Hemingway trick. He said to start by writing one true sentence about your character. Then another, then another. You dig yourself out of the hole of writer's block one sentence at a time.

What do you want readers to remember about your books?
That I had fun writing them.

What would you do if you ever stopped writing?
Sit on a beach and make up stories for my own amusement. Or if I were starting a new career from scratch, I'd study architecture.

What do you like best about yourself?
I have a big, loud laugh.

What do you consider to be your greatest accomplishment?
Raising a smart, empathetic, funny son.

What do you wish you could do better?
Exercise—I'm horrible and unmotivated!

What would your readers be most surprised to learn about you?
I'm a huge Three Stooges fan—I'm watching them now as I write this!

Martina and Bev are contestants in an online cupcake contest. But will Martina's sticker friends bake up trouble behind the scenes?

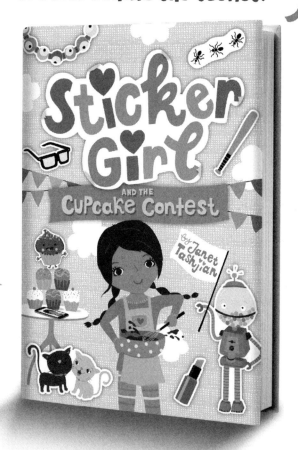

Don't miss the next Sticker Girl book!